The Other Planet Earth

by

K.J.Goss

SHIRES PRESS

4869 Main Street
P.O. Box 2200
Manchester Center, VT 05255
www.northshire.com

THE OTHER PLANET EARTH
©2020 by K.J. Goss

ISBN: 978-0-9997533-5-4

Building Community, One Book at a Time
*A family-owned, independent bookstore in
Manchester Ctr., VT, since 1976 and Saratoga Springs, NY since 2013.
We are committed to excellence in bookselling.
The Northshire Bookstore's mission is to serve as a resource for
information, ideas, and entertainment while honoring the needs
of customers, staff, and community.*

Printed in the United States of America

Cover design courtesy of Tina Grant, Northfield
,Vermont

This is dedicated to a very good friend, Pete,

who before his passing, I know would have

helped me in putting together this story

Chapter 1

Dan Morgan, a man in his early forty's, exited the elevator of the high-rise office building heading for his favorite park bench a few blocks away. Today, for whatever reason, felt different. He knew he was tense and today he was even frustrated. The rat race of the city he felt was slowly poisoning his mind and attitude. He was sure it wasn't his career work in photography. He loved his chosen work, just not the pressure of deadlines. They had an old saying from his military days of "Hurry up and wait." this seemed to apply more to today's world than it did to the military life. *"There has got to be a better way."* He thought to himself as he neared his bench.

He felt an annoyance flash through him when he saw another man sitting on "HIS" bench. *"That's got to be the tension."* he scolded himself. *"That man has every right in the world to be here."* Dan silently apologized to the man, sat down and proceeded to unwrap his meatloaf sandwich. He noticed the man gave a half smile and short nod as if acceptance of the apology. *"Just coincidence."* he said to himself again.

Dan watched the pigeons vying for the crumbs he threw while trying to force his thoughts to chill out. He did not understand what was going on with him. This was the third day this week his anxiety was getting the better of him. "*Life should not have to be complicated or demanding.*" he reasoned. *"Or perhaps it's just me."*

He finished his lunch and threw away his papers and turned back to the office.

"**H**ave a better day." His bench partner called after him.

Dan turned, nodded in recognition and went on his way.

"**T**hat's odd." he said aloud quietly. "It's as if he were reading my thoughts." Dan dismissed this idea. "It was most likely written on my face. There I go again." He thought, "Now I'm talking out loud to no one."

As soon as he reached his office and darkroom, he immersed himself in his trade. This appeared to be his only outlet for relief lately.

It was mid evening and dark when he finally left the building. He decided to walk home hoping to clear his head somewhat. Feeling a little relaxed by the time he got to his apartment he made a quick snack and fell right into bed.

The following day was no different than the last. The technical part of the job went well as always, if only he did not have to deal with people. Lunch was routine. He purchased a hot dog from a street vender and made his way to the park. His new bench buddy was there and nodded a greeting. Dan sat down ignoring the man and concentrated on the pigeons flocking at his feet. He let his mind drift to other times and places half wishing he could be there, but he had commitments to honor and to date he had never not honored his word. He could feel the presence of the man next to him slowly interfering with his thoughts.

"This shouldn't be happening." Dan told himself. *"I don't know this guy from Adam. I get the feeling I want to talk to him."*

He stood and walked a bit so he could observe his observer without making it too obvious. The man's dress was common, jeans, open collared denim shirt and well worn old cowboy boots. His face was pleasant enough and he wore a day or two's worth of unshaved whiskers. The man appeared to be writing in a small notebook, lifting his head now and then as if deep in thought.

Dan again dismissed his paranoid thoughts turning to head back to the office. Almost out of range he heard the man call after him;

"See you tomorrow." as if he was an old friend.

Dan chose to ignore this also, he had to get back to work.

He left work at a decent hour for a change which gave him time to prepare himself a regular dinner. A glass of wine with dinner helped the relaxation process even though his mind was still full from work related matters. Thoughts of his lunch time's unwanted companion crept in also.

"What is it about this man that is intriguing me so. I don't want to talk to him yet there is some thing of interest, that I can't identify, that is drawing me to perhaps find out why he intrigues me so."

Dan shook his head hoping that would shake the thoughts away. He poured a second glass of wine and turned on the television looking for distraction. Channel surfing brought him to an old Abbot and Costello "who done it" which worked. The movie was predictable but with enough comic spots to bring laughs. Work and lunch were soon forgotten, for now anyway.

Friday dawned with cloudy skies. *"No matter "* thought Dan, *"In order to meet this deadline I won't be going any place today except maybe a quick lunch break.*" His morning was non-stop and he welcomed the midday pause. Grabbing his thrown together sandwich he headed for the park. Dan approached his favorite bench cautiously to avoid his unwanted bench mate. "Great." he said out loud though quietly, "He's not here today, I can eat in piece."

He nibbled at the not so good sandwich giving most of it to the pigeons. Sitting back to relax for a while, Dan caught himself looking to the empty side of the bench.

"Why am I doing that. I'm glad he's not here. I have my privacy back again, so why do I feel like I'm missing something."

These thoughts were bothering Dan more than he wanted so he decided to cut his lunch short and go back to work. Walking back he focused his mind on the project he was working on. This seemed to help. The day was over before he knew it and he tried to think of plans for the weekend but could not come up with anything of real interest. He stopped for Chinese take out before going home. His mind was almost blank now and he just wanted to go home and "Veg" out.

He entered his apartment, threw the keys on the table and noticed the blinking light on his answering machine.

"Now what." he said annoyed as he pushed the button to retrieve the message.

"Dan, this is Mark Watson. The dead line has been moved up on the interior project by a week. I need the finals by Wednesday mid day. That's all for now, see you Wednesday."

Dan sighing deeply aloud, said ,

"Well now I know what my plans are for the weekend."

The message did not help his already agitated mood. Grabbing a beer and a fork he plopped in front of the TV and attacked his Egg Foo Yong.

Nine fifteen Saturday morning found Dan at his office stressing over the sudden change in dead lines.

"Why can't the world slow down some ? What's the big rush for, only to jump to the next thing and rush it also. I have to change." he emphasized to himself.

He put his mind back to the job in front of him.

"I will do something." he mumbled.

He worked non-stop and smoothly for the rest of the day not even breaking for lunch. Satisfied with his day's accomplishments he treated himself to dinner and went home to bed.

Chapter 2

The next few days were a maddening pace for Dan as he worked endlessly to meet the deadline. By Wednesday morning the completed project was set and ready for Mark. At eleven o'clock Mark showed up with a phony smile and his usual phony everything is wonderful attitude. Not wanting to get involved in his make believe world, Dan rushed Mark through the presentation making excuses that he had another appointment. The rush did not seem to bother Mark and he left as happy as he arrived. Dan was glad for this. As soon as Mark closed the door Dan swung into action securing all his equipment and turning out lights. Within minutes he was on his way to the park. He chatted with the local vender as he waited for his chile dog. Not caring about the chile dripping down the front of his shirt Dan made his way to his bench in the park paying little attention to anything. Just happy to be rid of the rush project he approached the bench only to find his unwanted visitor occupying the same corner. He thought about moving on and ignoring the man altogether when the stranger spoke;

"Quite a relief to get rid of the project wasn't it"

Dan looked at him oddly and said, "I beg your pardon, were you speaking to me."

"You know I was." said the man cheerfully. I sense some hostility in your voice. Why do you hesitate to talk to me. Down deep inside I know you want to."

Dan kept calm outwardly but his thoughts showed otherwise.

*"What is it about this stranger."*his thoughts rambling. *"He seems to know more about me than I know about myself."*

Deciding to get to the bottom of this Dan sat down , confronted the man directly asking;

"What do you want from me ? Why and how are you reading my mind ?

Feeling himself getting more annoyed, which he did not want to do, he continued,

"What gives you the right to invade my private and personal thoughts."

Dan stopped to get control of himself before he got too carried away. Calmly the stranger sat back and answered.

"To answer your first question first, It's not what I want from you, it's what you want from me."

Looking and feeling totally confused now, Dan replied,

"What do you mean, I want something from you, I don't even know you."

"That's okay, you will soon enough." smiled the stranger, "Secondly you allowed me to see your thoughts."

"I what ?" questioned Dan in a raised voice. Catching himself quickly he calmed back down.

"Let me further explain." the man replied still smiling. "You were concerned and made remarks about the world being too fast. How would you like to change that."

"How can I change that, I'm not in charge of millions of people." Dan questioned almost laughingly."

Retaining his smile the stranger sat back and quietly answered,

"You don't have to change the world but you can change the world you live in."

The stranger's comment interested Dan, but he did not know how to pursue it. He stared at his bench mate, his face free of expression.

"Ah ha !" the stranger acknowledged, "I see the thought of that premise intrigues you."

"I think that situation would intrigue any one but going about such a thing is just a pipe dream."

"Oh, you think so, well I guess we have no more to talk about then." answered the stranger. He made a motion as if to get up when Dan stopped him.

"No wait, please. What did you mean by what you said, you know, about changing the world I live in."

"It's not a pipe dream." The stranger answered finally showing some excitement. "Have you ever heard of an alternate existence or alternate world ?"

"Well- - - - ." Dan hesitated, "I remember reading articles about such a topic as alternate universes, but that was just hypothesizing. There was no facts presented to back up any of those crazy theory's."

"Ahh, but that's what you want to believe. You're afraid to think that such a thing may exist. Let me tell you sir that it does exist and is quite real."

The stranger gazed into Dan's eyes trying to show that he was telling the truth. He paused for a moment longer than stated firmly:

"I live in that world. Well, actually I live in both worlds. I pass from one to the other when I feel the need. And right now I feel that you could use my help."

"Your help in what ?" asked Dan without hesitation.

"Why to throw away the burden you're carrying .

You're a prime candidate for the other world.." answered the stranger.

"What burden ? What other world ? What are you talking about ?" Dan said, obviously annoyed at this man's forced meddling in his private thought's.

"No need to get upset sir." apologized the man. "Perhaps I should put this another way. To start with let me introduce myself properly." The stranger offered his hand saying "Ian Hathaway is the name and you are ?"

Dan extended his hand hesitantly. He did and did not want to know this man. He wanted his privacy back and yet some mysterious thing was pulling at him to seek more. More of what, he did not even know himself. Dan finally took the offered hand with a firm grasp and instantly felt a soft tingle start at the hand and slowly run through his whole body. A euphoria settled in and Dan was surprisingly relaxed. The two men exchanged remote smiles as they sat on the bench. The pigeons flocked to Dan as usual but this time were ignored. There would be no crumbs today.

"Now to clarify my earlier statement, if I may. As you said you have heard of the alternate world theory, you just don't believe it. I didn't either in the beginning."

"The beginning ?" questioned Dan, still feeling an almost non existent tingle.

"Yes." replied Ian. "You see many years ago I met a man who introduced me to another life. Well, not really another life, the same life but different in many ways."

"Now you're being confusing again." interrupted Dan.

"It may seem that way to you now so let me put it in plain and simple terms. An alternate world does exist. I live in it most of the time where I am free of the bothersome annoyances that you also appear to want to discard. I can help you get there Dan, just as someone helped me years ago. The decision is your's."

Wanting to, but not yet really believing what he just heard Dan remained silent. His gaze went to the pigeons while his mind was elsewhere. Ian sat back enjoying the day letting Dan have his time. Dan wanted to believe Ian, he admitted to himself. How often he had thought of getting away from it all. As crazy and frightening as this was perhaps the answer he longed for. After all Ian seemed to be enjoying being part of both worlds if this was really true. That would be like having your cake and eating it too.

Dan turned to Ian thinking;

"The existence of another world or parallel universe is a bit far fetched, even for me."

"I still have my doubts and misgivings but maybe I am interested in your proposal. However I feel more information is necessary."

Ian was both excited and disappointed at the same time.

"What more do you need my good man then to have your wish fulfilled. The other world is what ever you want it to be. You say you want your privacy and quiet without rush. There you shall have it. You still want to pursue your craft ? There you can take pictures till your hearts content. What ever you desire you will find. All you need to do is to wish it and think it and believe in what you wish for."

Ian was speaking with such animation one would think it was he who was going for the first time.

Ian's enthusiasm was contagious and Dan was seeing things he had wished for, for years. He looked around only to find he was no longer in the park. Ian was nowhere to be seen. Dan found himself on a country dirt road and not a soul in sight. To his right was a soft meadow filled with grass about knee high speckled here and there with wild flowers. A doe and her fawns were playing and chasing butterflies. Slowly walking he noticed a rambling brook to the left, it's serpentine meandering, weaving itself among trees of all kinds and sizes. The sun was leaving it's diamond sparkles on the water as it rushed over odd shaped rocks worn smooth by the water's action over time. The sweet song of unidentified birds filled the honey scented air. Dan walked to the stream seeing things he never noticed before. Things, he realized now, had always been there but were overlooked. The honey bees skipping from flower to flower, the dragon fly skimming the slow moving water, the jumping trout catching mosquito's while the frogs serenaded the water lily in his baritone voice. High above was a hawk circling in search of prey. A light breeze whispered through the tree tops, then caught the tall grasses bending them to his will.

Dan sat down by the water's edge, his back to a tree. He closed his eyes and listened to the noisy silence. He could not remember being this content or at peace with himself and the world about him. His eyelids slowly crept down shutting out the world he so longed for.

Dan Morgan awakened with a start only to find two rascally red squirrels playing tag while jumping over his feet. He gave a quiet hello only to surprise the pair who scurried up a nearby tree.

"Sorry." said Dan with a smile.

Moments later two little heads peeked around from behind the tree chattering as if scolding.

"I said I'm sorry." repeated Dan and laughed at his two companions.

They chattered some more then resumed their game of tag heading off who knows where.

Dan sat watching the stream a while longer his mind drifting to Ian's words.

"I'm definitely not in the park and honestly don't know how I got here. Am I really in an alternate place, or am I dreaming or worse yet hallucinating ? Am I going to wake up facing another deadline."

Not getting any answers Dan continued walking the country road. Off in the distance, green hills were reaching for the clouds drifting by.

Then something caught his attention at the base of the foot hills. It looked like a church spire interrupting the outline of the trees. He noticed other structures also. Dan resumed walking to the newly discovered village. Thirty minutes of a casual stride brought him to the edge of town. Here he saw people strolling the streets. It appeared to be a quaint little town with small shops painted a rainbow of colors. The road through town was dirt, but neat and well taken care of.

Curiosity pulled Dan further into town where he received friendly greetings from all who passed. At the center of the village was a circular green hosting a raised gazebo bandstand. The green itself was probably three acres he guessed. It was then he noticed other roads spoking out from the circle. They too were studded with multi colored buildings nothing over two story's.

Dan's mind reacted again;

"Why does this all look so familiar ? It's as if I were here before. It's all familiar and at the same time it's not."

An air of contentment overcame him.

"I like it here." he said aloud.

"We all do." came a voice from behind.

Dan turned to find a young woman smiling at him.

He smiled back saying;

"I'm sorry. You must think I'm some kind of nut standing here talking to myself."

"Not at all she replied smiling. We are all here for the same reason. To forget the rat race."

This statement registered instantly with Dan.

"Perhaps I'm not crazy and perhaps Ian was genuine." He thought.

Not knowing what else to say he asked,

"Have you been here long."

He then scolded himself.

"What a stupid thing to say, this is not a pickup bar." he whispered in his mind.

"I only started coming here about a year and a half ago." she answered. "I just had to get out of the rat race of the city."

"A familiar refrain." Dan replied.

"I don't think I've seen you here before. Is this your first time ?"

"Does it show that much ?" Dan returned.

"No need to feel self conscious." she smiled. "We're all here for the same reason. If you're anything like me, you'll love it here. In fact you may not want to go back."

Perplexed by her comment Dan inquired,

"Is that possible ?"

"Of course." she answered instantly. "There are quite a few people who live here permanently. I myself plan to make that same move sometime in the next few month's"

Surprised by this, Dan, puzzled, asked;

"What about friends and family, where you work, where you live ? You can't just up and disappear ?"

"Of course you can't." she laughed in answer, but there are methods to enact this. I assume you're here through Ian ?"

Dan stuttered a yes answer, looking at her questioningly.

Now her smile was polite.

"It's not my place to say anymore but you can take that up with Ian. I'm sure he will be more than happy to provide answers to what ever questions you have. I must go now, it was a pleasure to meet you."

She turned and briskly walked away.

"But wait !" Dan yelled after her to no avail. She was already out of ear shot.

Dan stood frozen in place for a while trying to make sense of what was happening. He walked to the gazebo on the green and sat down on the steps. He had to think. The last thing he remembered was sitting in the park bench with Ian. Dan closed his eyes, shook his head gently to dislodge the cobwebs. He sensed a presence, opened his eyes and saw Ian sitting next to him on his favorite park bench in his favorite city park.

Chapter 3

"How was it." Ian asked accompanied by a broad grin.

Dan took a moment to readjust and slowly answered;

"Serene and quiet."

"Well isn't that what you wanted ?" quizzed Ian.

"Yes, but." Dan hesitated looking for the right words. "I was pleased and content for a time, but I was also frightened and confused. Perhaps frightened is the wrong word, I guess disturbed would be more appropriate. How did I get there ? Was it real ? Was I hypnotized ? How did I get back here.?"

Dan put his head down to his hands, his elbows resting on his knees, shaking his head gently back and forth.

"Now I know I chose the right person." Ian said quietly.

"What do you mean, chose the right person." Dan questioned looking at Ian, eyes filled with curiosity.

"I'm sure you're confusions will go away when you understand more." volunteered Ian matter of factly.

"That would be great." Dan answered sternly. "I attempted to get some understanding from a young woman I met but was hastily put off. She mentioned you and that you would explain whatever I needed to know."

"That I can do my friend, that is if you are truly prepared to receive and accept that information."

"What do you mean accept ? Accept what ? What is this big secret ?"

Dan had raised his voice slightly, showing his annoyance with this word game.

"I'm sorry to have upset you, my friend, and yes I owe you a full explanation. Please relax and listen and I will reveal all and answer all of your curiositys. Trust me it will be worth it."

"I certainly hope so." snapped Dan, still slightly annoyed. "Right now I need some stability and structure so I know what direction I'm going with my life."

Ian chuckled lowly.

"Relax my friend and listen."

Dan agreed to give Ian a chance because deep inside he really wanted this to be true.

To start with I will undeniably state that there is definitely an alternate Planet Earth . In fact there is a complete alternate universe. Just about a mirror image."

Dan interrupted immediately.

"How come I haven't heard of this before ? Why is this generally not known ?"

"I can answer that also." Ian answered calmly. "You see the scientific world deals strictly in classical documented facts, not hearsay or suppositions. They have not yet figured out how to physically get there, there fore it does not exist. I know that sounds cruel for me to say it that way, but it's true. I believe there are some scientific minds who accept an alternate world theory but fail to pursue it without documentation. Factual documentation. Their careers hang on the balance of that. Hence it does not get studied."

"That sounds rather short sighted." commented Dan.

"That may be." smiled Ian in answer, "But that's also a fact of life."

"How is it then, that you are aware of such an alternate world and even universe ?" challenged Dan.

"Ah! Now we are getting to the heart of the matter." answered Ian, his enthusiasm building. "An open mind is the answer. I have always kept an open mind. Believe it or not Dan, this vagrant like figure sitting before you is really a recognized astronomer. An astronomer astro- physicist to be exact. Early on in my career I had this gut feeling about an alternate universe and was almost laughed out of my profession. It was then I learned the art of secrecy for survival."

Dan was staring at the man before him surprise and shock apparently written all over his face. Dan stuttered out,

"But H-H How did - - - when did you - - - How, how did this come about ? When did you know this existed ? This other world ?"

"Well, as I said my gut feel led to extensive detailed research. Access to previous research was also invaluable. Actually my biggest and most welcome breakthrough was meeting someone who was already enjoying the benefits of both worlds."

"You mean like me meeting you ?" interjected Dan.

"Exactly." returned Ian.

"What's this about an open mind." asked Dan.

Ian continued; "Aside from my own feeling, the research studies I was pursuing were indicating this phenomena existed. For one with a closed, scientific, fact only mind, research avenues like mine were totally rejected, hence the need for continued secrecy. The man who found me, quite accidentally I might add, had followed the same line of thinking as my research that led to his discovery at an earlier time."

"You said you met accidently ?" Dan inquired further.

"Yeah!" Ian laughed, "We met at a cocktail lounge one evening and just started chatting and discovered our mutual interest. That being, an open mind and more to your liking, a less frantic world. To focus on the open mind part for a moment, it is this acceptance of things we do not fully understand or have technical background enough to understand that makes it seem mysterious. Personally I do not find these things to be mysterious. I believe there are yet undiscovered phenomena that exist and always have existed. Perhaps some day we will see them revealed also, but for now let us concentrate on the other world that is possibly better for us then the one we live in now."

Ian paused a moment then asked,

"I hope that clears up any misgivings you may have had."

"It does explain a lot, I think. However, that still leaves the question of how did I get there and more puzzling, how did I get back ?"

Ian was laughing again a little more heartily this time.

"That's the advantage of an open mind , an open and welcoming mind. Never let go of that instinct and asset. It will always serve you well.

A puzzled look now shadowing his face Dan questioned;

"You mean to tell me that it is my own mind or thoughts that allow me to transport myself from one world to another ?"

"Yes." answered Ian, it is that simple as long as you believe that the other world exists than you can transport there."

"You mean it's just a mind game ?" asked Dan.

"Far from it and it is anything but a game." replied Ian. "You actually physically travel there through the use of your mind.

Trying to sort this out further for his own satisfaction Dan required more information.

"I don't mean to belabor the point, but based on what you are saying, if I transport to the alternate world it is not just mental but physically as well ?" If I am in the other world I am not still physically present in this world. Is that correct ?"

"That is exactly correct." commented Ian. "I'm thinking you need further convincing. Let's perform an experiment right now. We'll first wait for this couple to pass us. This is something you will learn soon enough. When ever you are going to transport make sure no one is around. Not all understand such things. Once the man and woman were out of sight Ian said; "Okay now!"

Dan watched intently as Ian closed his eyes, his face was overcome with obvious serious concentration. Dan sat open mouthed as Ian just slowly faded away. Dan sat alone for a moment staring at the empty bench seat. Finally regaining composure he reached out to where Ian had been sitting. It was truly empty space. Ian was physically absent.

Two women were approaching from the garden path so Dan, not to look like a total jerk, picked up the newspaper Ian left and pretended he was searching through the pages. Luckily the two women ignored his presence and were soon out of sight. A few more minutes passed and Ian reappeared standing behind the bench.

"I did not want to chance sitting on top of somebody." he said smiling. "Are you convinced now ? You are truly transported to another place."

"I guess I'm convinced." Dan said hesitantly. "At least I think I am. It's just so strange, the concept of whole beings being transported with only the use of the mind is just weird."

Ian answered with a laughing "You'll get used to it."

"NO, let's get serious for the moment." Dan said. "I'd like to know what actually takes place. How do we physically get from one place to the other. I feel I should know, or rather I feel I want to know."

Ian answered in a serious tone;

"That's something we all would like to know."

Dan looked at Ian with a surprised and confused expression.

"You mean to tell me that you don't know how it's done that we just do it."

"That's precisely what I'm saying." was Ian's answer. As if in explanation he continued; "I'm sure you are aware that the human mind is one of the most powerful and complete forces in the universe and I might add, the least understood. Today's science, with all it's so called advanced technology, cannot fathom or even come near explaining such happenings, therefore, most don't even try."

"How did you get involved ?' Dan inquired.

"Well, like you I have always believed in things you can't see. There are inexplicable forces at work out there. A few of us have been fortunate enough to tap into their grids and over century's have had the benefit and advantage of enjoying things most folk don't even know exist. In my small opinion it boils down to one thing, having an open and accepting mind and allowing yourself to think beyond any society made boundaries, old or new."

Dan thought about this for a few minutes, then asked,

"Not to belabor this discussion, but - - - this alternate world or universe, how far away is it ? How much distance are we actually traversing ?"

"I knew you would get around to that sooner or later."smiled Ian. "I hate to admit it but that's an unknown factor even to us that enjoy the other world. It's more of a mind thing, though we are physically moving the corporal body. The alternate universe just exists. I'm sure it has always existed. Some people call it a parallel universe but that still does not identify a measured distance. As I said it's a mind thing and at the same time it is very real."

"**I**'m convinced, finally, that it is a real thing having experienced it myself." stated Dan. "However there is still one thing that intrigues me. Those persons who choose to stay there permanently , what about their life in this universe ? How is that handled ? I mean as far as relatives and friends, jobs and housing ? You can't just disappear without some sort of repercussion or consequences. What happens with that ?

Ian sat back with his half smile saying;

"**I** wish I could answer that for you, but you can probably figure that out for yourself as well as I can."

Looking somewhat confused Dan answered;

"**W**ell I do have my own thoughts on that but that's just it, they are my own thoughts on the possibilities of accomplishing such a thing. At least how I myself would go about it."

"**T**hen that's your answer. As you said it is an individual thing, each of us would have his own method and reasons."

Dan challenged in return, "The remaining mystery, which could be a problem, is the government. What do we do about tax records and other records of identification. As I stated earlier, You can't just disappear."

"No I guess you can't." replied Ian. "I know a few that have, but they died in order to do it."

Ian saw Dan's expression change and immediately added;

"At least they made it appear that way. This way all records would stop and they were free to do what they wanted."

Dan understood this. He himself had considered it as one of his options.

"Most people though consider the alternate world as R&R. They constantly travel back and forth between the two worlds. It's more like a vacation getaway. I can see you're creating a problem for your self."

"What do you mean." asked Dan.

"Well, it looks as if you are contemplating a permanent move but are wondering what happens later on if you change your mind and want to go back to your original world. Am I correct ?"

"The thought did occur to me." answered Dan.

"All your decisions are your own and I will not influence them in any way but I will advise you not to make any hasty moves. Take your time to consider all options. Your alternate world will always be there. It always was."

Chapter 4

Dan, deep in confused thoughts, suddenly realized Ian was no longer with him.

"Just as well." he thought, *"I need some alone time."*

He sat back down on his favorite bench and let his mind wander. In fact he gave up completely of even thinking of anything specific as he watched the pigeons pecking at microscopic crumbs scattered on the ground before him.

"Talk about a simple life." he laughed to himself, *"Eat crumbs people throw at you and poop on statues. How less involved can you get."*

Dan's gaze shifted upwards and he watched a few white cotton ball wisps slowly drift by. They reminded him of his short visit to the other planet Earth, and so the thoughts started again.

While he was talking with Ian all his remarks materialized as negative or problematic.

"Perhaps I should concentrate on what would be the positive aspects." Dan thought. *"And what better way to do that is there than being there."*

Dan closed his eyes and pictured the quant village he was in on his first visit.

~ ~ ~ ~ ~ ~

"Well, hello again." said a pleasant female voice.

"It's nice to see you again. Do you plan on staying longer this time ?" she asked smiling.

With his eyes fully opened now he saw the same woman he spoke with last visit. Now he studied her more closely. He found her to be quite attractive, poised in her demeanor, yet openly friendly in her mannerisms. Her medium length light brown hair framed a classic beauty face whose skin appeared to be flawless. Her smile was contagious and made her eyes twinkle with genuine warmth. Her figure was not hard on his eyes either. This observation took only seconds and Dan was glad of that. He did not want to appear rude by staring at her.

Remembering her question Dan replied with a smile;

"I needed time to think and a quiet place to do it."

Not seeming to be annoyed she softly answered,

"Then I will just leave you to your thoughts. Perhaps we will meet again at a more convenient time."

As she turned to go Dan rushed to answer;

"Please stay."

He felt embarrassed by giving her the wrong impression.

"I want you to stay. You can help by answering some remaining questions." Then he added another "Please."

With another of her pleasant and winning smiles she replied,

"Then I will be more than happy to stay kind sir and since you are now obviously ready for answers I will try to provide them for you. Come and walk with me. There is a lovely little café down the street that serves the most delicious coffee. There we can talk without interruption.

Her smile and invitation were irresistible, so down the road they went like two giddy school children.

She was right, the coffee was excellent and the café was a quaint home like setting. They sat at a window table enjoying the view of the center of town.

"I guess we should make it official." she said as she extended her hand across the table. "My name is Daria. Daria Collins, and you are ?"

Daniel Morgan. Dan to most people."

Her hand was soft and warm and their clasp lingered more than it should have, caught up in the moment.. The appearance of the waitress with pastry's broke the temporary spell and they both sheepishly withdrew their hands.

Dan looked up at the waitress who was staring at him with a warm smile and a curious "I'd like to know you better." look in her eyes. He dismissed this as his imagination

"These pastry's are a wonderful compliment to the coffee." Daria said breaking off a small piece from the one on her plate.

Smiling again she continued; "Now that we have been officially introduced perhaps I can answer some questions you obviously have."

Feeling comfortable with his new acquaintance Dan returned the smile and softly answered,

"Perhaps you can. Just before I arrived here Ian and I had quite a long session. I have a much better understanding now but pieces are still missing." Dan hesitated for a moment then inquired, "May I ask you a direct question ?"

"Sure, why not." answered Daria.

"Are you here permanently or do you travel back and forth."

"And here I thought it was going to be a difficult question." Daria smiled in answer. "Right now I go back and forth, but I am contemplating moving here permanently. I like it here, it pleases me to be here."

Dan remained silent for a moment gazing out the window. Daria understood Dan's thoughts having been through the same thing herself not too long ago, so she let him have his time.

Facing Daria once again, Dan spoke:

"That's exactly one of the missing pieces. Aside from being a less stressful world, what are the differences ? What do you do for money ? Is there a government ? What do you do about conflict ? How is it kept stress free ? Is it that easy to give up an already established life ?" Dan hesitated again. "Forgive me for boring you. I'm sure you have better things to do than to listen to some idiot rambling."

"On the contrary Dan." Daria answered seriously. "Your rambling's or feelings more correctly, are the same as everyone else who has ever entered this world. Those questions can stir up a lot in one's mind and yet we still chose to be here. It's not an easy decision but if you decide to be here I do believe you will have no regrets. That being said I think I may be able to answer a lot of questions."

Dan's spirit picked up but was dashed again when Daria added,

"But there is one caveat."

Dan's eyes questioned her.

"It can only be over dinner this evening." she said with a big smile.

Taken completely by surprise Dan stuttered an answer with a growing grin.

"I'm starting to like it here already and yes I would like very much to dine with you this evening."

"Wonderful." she said lightly touching his hand. I'll call for you about seven then."

A slight frown crossed Dan's face as he spoke again.

"But wait a minute, I have no place to stay, I'm totally new here. This visit was not exactly planned."

"That's an easy problem to solve." Daria answered happily. "There's an Inn with separate cabins just on the edge of town. The cabins are set aside for just this purpose, for first or second time visitors like you, an unplanned visit. There is no cost to you at all.

This program allows people the time necessary to make the decisions you are now facing. And even then there is no rush in that process. Sorry, I have to run now. I have an appointment, but I will see you at seven." said a smiling Daria. "Remember, just down the road. It's called the Worry Free Inn."

She got up and gracefully walked away. He finished the last swallow of coffee and went to the counter to settle the bill and was told everything had been taken care of. He thanked the lady with the warm inviting eyes and went out to face the sunshine.

Chapter 5

The Worry Free Inn was a charming old farmhouse complete with rockers on the shaded porch surrounded by well placed large Oak trees to keep the sun out but let the cool breeze flow freely. One hundred or so feet away were a half dozen small log cabins, each with it's own porch that held both hammock and rocking chairs.

Dan checked in with just his signature and was directed to the very last cabin overlooking a brook fed pond fading back to the forest. The inside was rustic though warmly appointed, consisting of a sitting room complete with fire place, a small bedroom and a quaint little kitchenette fully stocked. These total surroundings put one instantly at ease. He drifted out to the porch and eased himself into the rocker allowing the sense of peace to take over his consciousness. The setting directed his mind to this feeling of a Shangra La as he listened to the soft breeze and babbling brook.

Dan's eyes grew heavy but was quickly startled back to reality. His brain was buzzing again. Part of him was fighting this euphoria. "How can I live here. I have no job, no money, and no where to live. How does one survive here. Dan could feel his anxiety building. Is this place unique or is this really a whole planet ? Are there still other country's and other peoples.

Dan calmed himself thinking of Daria. She promised answers. Apparently he dozed off, which was understandable given the setting, because suddenly he found himself looking at six o' clock.. He reluctantly left the peaceful setting and went inside to shower. Finding a comfortable set of clean clothes he finished dressing just in time to hear a soft knock at the door.

Daria looked absolutely radiant. Her attire was nothing fancy, in fact it was rather plain which just enhanced her wholesome attractiveness.

"I chose a quaint little steak house about twenty miles out of town. The setting is simple but the menu is superb." Daria volunteered.

"Sounds good." Dan answered as he closed the door behind them.

Her car was nameless but looked similar to all those manufactured today. They chatted about nothing in particular on the way to the restaurant, though Dan did enjoy the view, both outside and inside the car.

"Watch it boy, don't get too interested, at least not just yet." he thought to himself.

The restaurant was just what she said it would be. Elegantly simple with a menu that would tempt any critic. They ordered a bottle of wine and as they sipped Dan was anxious with questions.

"I know you're bursting with curiosity so start your questions and I'll see if I can get you satisfied." Daria said.

"I guess I'll start with the obvious, at least to me, they're obvious." Dan replied.

"Go on " she smiled.

"This probably sounds foolish but is this really an actual parallel planet. Or is it just one little town which could be a figment of my imagination."

Daria smiled again in a very comfortable way.

"It's not a foolish question at all. In fact I think it's quite logical. I had very similar thoughts myself when I first came here. To answer your question, yes it is a real planet, with real country's and real people."

"**W**hat about the people ? In other words what's the population count." Dan pushed.

"**I** said this is as real as you can see. The total population is only about twenty percent of where you came from, world wide that is. Of course it varies from country to country." Daria answered

"***S**omething didn't sound right. He couldn't pin point anything, he just felt uncomfortable about the answer. Yes, she answered the question, but he felt something was missing. Sincerity I think.*" Dan thought to himself. He did not show his discomfort and decided to ask further questions. He didn't know why but something inside urged him to put up a front saying,

"**W**ow! That sounds great. I could use a world with less people."

Daria beamed her winning smile again.

"**W**hat about a job, money and housing ? I'm a stranger here, so how does one settle here ? That is if I decide to stay."

Dan's last statement triggered just a minuscule change in her eyes. It only lasted for a split second but that same bell in his head tingled slightly. Daria continued well composed.

"**Y**ou're a photographer right, I'm sure you will have no problem setting up a business here. It will be no different than in the other world. Perhaps you would prefer one of the bigger cities such as where you work now. As far as the money is concerned it is exactly the same. If you have any savings in the other world just bring it with you. An account can be established here."

"And housing ?" Dan inquired.

Apartments and houses are always available. You could even make arrangements to have something custom built if you prefer."

"There was still something missing in her answer." he thought. *"For now I'll just continue to play along."*

Dan changed the subject for the moment and asked about the weather. Daria almost looked relieved to discuss something as general as that.

They ordered dinner and continued with small talk. During dessert Dan returned to serious questions.

"What's the government like here, you know taxes, regulations etc ?"

She hesitated for a moment as if looking for the right answer.

"The governments here are slightly different. The structure is pretty much the same but they operate better and only do what is agreed upon by the people."

"You mean like a true republic." Dan remarked.

That slight hesitation showed itself again.

"I guess you could say that."

Dan could tell she was becoming uncomfortable so he immediately switched subjects again.

"Well I must say, you certainly know how to pick a restaurant."

A relieved expression lit up her face and she smiled her irresistible smile.

"I guess she did not anticipate the questions I asked." Dan thought to himself. They went back to trivial discussions to finish out the evening.

Dan decided he would try one more question before she dropped him off.

"What about travel ? Suppose I wanted to go to France for the week ?"

"Travel is pretty much the same and it's okay as long as you get permission." Daria answered.

"Permission ! Why do I need permission" Dan said in a raised voice questioningly.

Recovering quickly she added;

"You know what I mean, that you have a passport and the like."

Dan could feel her nervousness and continued to play along as if nothing had happened.

"Oh right, a passport, of course. I don't know what I was thinking."

She let out a phony laugh but it was obvious to see she was relieved. Dan decided not to push the questions any further on this night.

They had now arrived back at "The Worry Free Inn".

Daria stopped at the entrance drive making no indication about going any closer to the cabin. Dan politely asked,

"Will I see you tomorrow, I may have more questions that you could probably answer for me."

"S..s..s sure." She stumbled in answer. "I have an appointment tomorrow morning, but I can meet you at the coffee house about mid-morning. Shall we say about ten thirty or so."

"Fine." agreed Dan. "That will give me some time to walk around town and see the sights."

With that said, Dan exited the car, waved good bye as she hurriedly drove away. Dan walked to his assigned cabin and sat in the porch rocker for awhile. He needed time to think undisturbed.

Chapter 6

The wine at dinner had Dan a little mellow, not really inebriated, more of a relaxed state you would say, but not near enough to stop his mind from questions. Questions about the answers Daria was giving. Why did he have this constant alarm bell going off regarding her answers ? He detected an uneasiness in her answers. What was she trying to hide ? He certainly didn't feel threatened but he knew, or at least had a gut feel that something was not right. He didn't think that she caught on that he was suspicious of her answers but she was uncomfortable with his questions. He made up his mind to continue playing dumb and innocent. "Lets see what tomorrow will bring." he said quietly aloud.

He let his mind drift to the night sky for a while, and then to an upcoming photo shoot before finally falling into bed.

Up with the sun and feeling quite rested, Dan slept well in spite of everything going on in his mind. Having made himself coffee he wandered out to the porch to the rocker, mug in hand.

"I wonder what's in store today." He thought.

Trying not to let it bother him too much now he answered himself.

"I just have to wait and see."

Finishing his coffee he showered and set out for the cafe' and breakfast. The same lovely waitress greeted him with her warm smile. For a moment Dan thought he detected a very happy you're back glint in her eyes. He placed his order and watched her walk away thinking how poised and attractive she was, even without her smile. He read the newspaper while eating noting that there was no real news. Nothing bad or even questionable, only happy articles.

"Strange." he thought. *"But in a way I guess that's refreshing for a change."*

Just as Dan was ready to leave Daria walked in accompanied by a man

"I thought I'd find you here." She said smiling and without pausing she added, "This is Ted Larson." pointing to her companion. "Ted this is Dan Morgan, the man I was telling you about."

The two men shook hands and exchanged smiles.

"Can we sit and talk for a while Dan, I think Ted can answer all of your questions better than I could, that's why I brought him along."

"Sure why not." Dan answered, "I don't really have anything planned for the day."

"Oh good." Smiled Daria beaming as usual.

Coffee was ordered all around and Ted took over the conversation. He spoke very casually but Dan still detected a guarded air about the man.

"So! Daria tells me you're interested in losing the rat race like the rest of us here. It can sure make a difference in your life style. It's nice to be stress free."

"It sounds almost too good to be true." Dan said in a half laugh trying not to have them put their guard up too much. "I still have a few questions though."

"Fire away Dan, I'm sure I can help you out." Ted replied.

"What about money ? I will need a job and a place to live, a house preferably ?"

Ted jumped right in.

"Well being a photographer should get you a job easily. Small towns can always use a studio, or if you prefer there's always a newspaper or magazines. How about a wildlife magazine ?"

"That sounds like just what I want." Dan said animatedly. "I always wanted to do more work outdoors rather than in a stuffy office building."

He looked for reactions from both Ted and Daria. He got what he wanted. His enthusiasm settled them both. He knew their guard was now relaxed. Dan now continued with easy questions.

"What about money ? Can I bring money with me from my present home ?"

"You can if you want." answered Ted. "It will be accepted here, but it really isn't necessary."

"How do you mean not necessary ?" Dan inquired still keeping a dumb and friendly look about him.

"Well our system of exchange here is different." explained Ted.. "What ever amount you would bring here would be deposited in the general account that one draws from. You see everything here is pretty much equal, that way we eliminate the greed factor which in turn fosters peace and harmony. Without that push to out do the other guy we maintain this stress free environment."

"But doesn't that eliminate competition." Dan pushed further.

"Exactly." Answered Ted immediately taking control of the conversation again. "There is no need for competition. Everybody shares in each others success and that success is good for the whole community."

Dan hesitated for a moment, his mind racing putting all these pieces together. He again searched their eyes and was pleased to see no sign of alert. Not yet anyway.

"What do you consider the community? This small town?"

"Oh no." said Ted. It could be the state or part of a state, or a combination of states or actually the whole nation. The community is an ever changing body. The fluctuation is needed to keep the success and harmony equal. For example someone's fruitful success in California benefits everyone's community accounts. This way we're always equal. So you see money is really not a very important factor."

Dan accepted this explanation willingly, not to raise suspicions. His mind was really processing this information to put together a more thorough picture of what was driving this world of no stress, if you wanted to call it that. *"Ted was becoming more animated now."* thought Dan. *"He is totally immersed into his subject "*It was obvious Ted wanted to keep going so Dan let him have his reins.

"**W**e really don't use money per se' here. Everyone is issued an equal amount of credit each month and that's what you use to purchase goods and services. Should you find yourself with credits over your monthly allotment because of a successful venture or project you sold, you are expected to spend them. This keeps our economy always funded and flowing. It remains strong and we all share in that financial strength, hence less stress and therefore happy and at peace."

*"**A**nd your individuality disappears. "*Dan thought to himself while keeping an outward smile on his face. "Wow !, that sounds unique." he said aloud not meaning a word of it. "Not to change the subject but what about travel ? You know a change of scenery or a yearning to see something or someplace else now and then."

"**T**ravel, ah, oh yes." Ted answered looking somewhat lost. "Yes of course there's travel but most choose not to travel. Everyone seems content with who and where they are. You do realize having a stress free life will make all the difference in the world on your outlook and future life."

"What a bunch of hogwash." ran through Dan's mind.

"But you can go to the airport, buy a ticket and fly to Europe if you so choose." Dan questioned calmly while smiling.

"Well not exactly." joined Daria. "You see there is really no need to go to Europe. Everything you could possibly want or need is provided for you right here."

"In other words you're saying I'm not allowed ?"

Dan knew he was now getting to both of them. For the moment they were at a loss for words. Ted spoke up but you could see he was deep in thought.

"Of course you're allowed, it's just that it's not done that often. Most people are content to just stay put."

Dan felt he was reaching for words but really wasn't saying anything. He did not want to set off too many alarms, at least not yet, so he decided to play along some more.

"Well perhaps you're right. There is something to be said for being content and happy."

This seemed to satisfy them both for now. Daria relaxed a bit and smiled..

"Is there anything else we can clarify for you."

Trying to keep it low key Dan answered with;

"I don't think so right now. Who knows perhaps later, right now I think I would like to take a walk and enjoy the rest of the day. There appears that there is a lot I would like to see."

"Of course." answered Daria. "Go right ahead , enjoy yourself. Perhaps we can meet again tomorrow."

Ted smiled, extended his hand again, "Nice to have met you Dan. I look forward to a long friendship."

Dan shook his hand as they stood. They both seemed anxious to get away from him. He was not at all surprised at that.

Dan took his time finishing his coffee to give Ted and Daria plenty of time to get away. He needed his own alone time also. What started out to be a great idea was becoming extremely complicated. Finally draining his coffee cup he wandered out to face the sunshine. He let the beautiful countryside occupy his mind for a while before engaging questions and explanations once again.

I imagine one could be content here for a while, but not forever. he thought .

A few hours spent exploring were enough for now, it was time to put his brain in high gear and figure just what this place was.

Arriving back at his cabin, Dan freshened up and poured himself a beer and settled in the rocker once more.

"What is it about this place that makes me feel so ill at ease." He asked himself. *"Something was just not right."*

Before Dan got too deep in thought the Inn manager walked by. They exchanged pleasantries and worked into normal chit chat. He decided to try a few questions, asked of course in all innocense.

"It's so peaceful here and appears to be trouble free, but what about the local crime rate ? Do you have the usual trouble makers like any other town ?"

"No, not at all." Replied Josh the Inn manager. "It's not really allowed."

"Ah haa!" thought Dan. *"I hit pay dirt. There's that same phrase again, not allowed. But I must continue to play the innocent to see where it takes me. Perhaps I'll get some real answers. Correct answers."*

Dan focused on the manager stating, with a smile;

"That's convenient, no wonder it's so peaceful. Wouldn't it be nice if that were everywhere."

"It pretty much is." answered Josh. "At least in the places I've been."

"You mean the trouble making kind just aren't here. Not enough excitement for them I guess." Dan said in an almost disinterested tone.

"No, that's not what I mean." remarked Josh. "There have been a number of those kind who have managed to cross over but once identified they are dealt with right away."

Dan paused then decided to push the issue. He needed answers.

"What do you mean dealt with ?"

"That's just it, no one really knows. They're not seen or heard of again." replied Josh willingly.

"Maybe they are sent back to the world we all started from." Dan offered innocently.

"I doubt it." Josh replied quickly, then added, "Look I've said too much already. I have other things to attend to. I must go now."

He stood up and turned to leave. Dan rushed to say:

"Wait, you just can't leave me hanging." He went ahead and risked additionally : "I have other things that disturb me, that perhaps you could shed more light on.

Josh looked around in a nervous manner.

"Tonight, in your cabin, after midnight. Leave your lights off." he whispered and rushed away.

Dan sat alone now, somewhat bewildered. He knew he questioned this other planet scenario and thought for awhile it was just his own doubts and wild imagination. He hoped he would be wrong with the doubts, but now perhaps there was confirmation of his thoughts. Instead of comfortable acceptance of his situation his suspicions were gaining credibility. *"What have I gotten myself into."* he thought. *"Perhaps I should return now to the rat race and forget about this whole thing. If I can get back."* he questioned. *"No."* Dan answered himself. *"I've got to pursue this till I get some real answers. But answers to what I don't even know. With any luck there will be a logical explanation to my suspicions and I can go on with my normal life. I must not jump to conclusions without proper information. Maybe I can clear my mind till I talk to Josh tonight. I think I saw a vending machine near the office when I checked in, I could use a snack to go with the beer."*

Returning with a bag of chips Dan grabbed another beer and headed for the brook. A short nap under a tree seemed like a great idea.

Chapter 7

As requested Dan turned the lights off in the cabin. He actually did that by eleven o'clock to appear as if he was asleep. There was a light rain that evening when Dan heard a quiet tap on the door. It all seemed very James Bond-ish. Josh whispered his name and Dan responded quickly in opening the door. Josh begged a moment to adjust his eyes to the dark then spotted a chair and seated himself.

Dan started off immediately by asking;

"What did you mean this afternoon when you said those people were not heard of again."

"Just what I said." Josh replied nervously. "Look, there are a lot of things going on here that you are not supposed to question and that's one of them. You're supposed to abide by the rules and behave. You are free to do whatever they want you to do and nothing more."

"**A**nd who is the they ?" Dan questioned.

"**I** don't know." Josh replied. "I don't think the average person knows. I don't think *"THEY"* want you to know."

"**W**hat about travel." inquired Dan. "Are you or are you not allowed to go places. I spoke to a gentleman by the name of Ted this morning. He was very evasive. I didn't really get an answer at all."

"**A**nd you probably won't" interrupted Josh. "I'm not sure but he may be one of the they."

Dan smiled to himself while asking;

"**H**ow do you know I'm not one of them."

"**I**'ve been here long enough to know who isn't the them, I haven't been able to figure exactly who is though." Josh replied apparently more comfortable now.

"**W**hat exactly is going on here." asked Dan curiously.

"**I** wish I knew." replied Josh. "But I'm glad to meet someone else with doubts. Perhaps between the two of us we can make some sense of this place."

"**D**o you know of any other doubters." Dan continued.

"**N**ot locally that I know of, but I did meet a man in England I suspect would be aligned with us. He also was new like you to this alternate world." Josh answered. "Which reminds me, you still have the chance to escape. If I were you I would take it."

Puzzled by this statement Dan pushed further.

"Don't you still have the option to leave ? You almost sound as if you couldn't or were not allowed."

"The latter is probably closer to the truth than you think."

This answer peaked Dan's curiosity even further yet.

"What do you mean "Not allowed." he asked in a non believing tone. Then it dawned on him.

"So that's the partial secret of this place." he mumbled aloud.

"You hit it right my friend." Josh said quietly. "It seems like they're recruiting. For what again I don't know. That part still remains a secret to me."

Dan then asked as if thinking out loud,

"So in other words you're saying that if I wanted to go to let's say the Middle East to visit that I wouldn't be allowed."

"That's about it." answered Josh. "They would not out right forbid it, but there would be so many obstacles put in your way you would eventually give up."

"And if I persisted ?" furthered Dan.

"Well let's put it this way, I did hear of a few people who pushed the envelope and suddenly they went on vacation. It's funny though, they never came back." Josh said sarcastically.

"So since I'm basically new here I can still go back to my original world no questions asked, but if I decide to stay then I'm here for good." stated Dan.

"That's about it." sighed Josh. "Not only here for good but your travel here is also limited. The choice is your's my friend. If I were you I'd get out now. Look, I've been here long enough for tonight, I don't want to be spotted. Let me know what you decide and perhaps we can meet again. Leave the lights out and if I don't see you again, don't worry. I'll understand."

Josh got up and quietly walked to the door.

"Good luck" he whispered as he quickly exited.

Dan remained quiet starring at the empty darkness. He wanted to think about what had just transpired, yet part of him did not want to put forth the effort. He just sat there in a numb like trance.

Chapter 8

The sun filtered through the curtains only to find Dan still glued to the chair he was in the night before. The sound of the birds early morning song slowly nudged him awake. He shifted position in the chair only to feel the results of a most uncomfortable night. His neck ached and his spine thought it had been hit by a train. Nothing seemed to want to work right. He relaxed a bit hoping to regain some sense of stability. Eventually the world came into focus and his muscles decided to cooperate but not without complaints.

Dan almost didn't remember last night or maybe didn't want to. He made some coffee and decided he would return to his real world. There, he felt he could do some uninfluenced thinking. While rinsing his cup the phone rang. He let it ring four times before answering. As he suspected it was Daria, her voice all peaches and cream. He lied about a deadline for a job back in the other world and that he would have to leave for a few days. He expected her sudden silence and could detect the caution in her tone as she answered that she understood and admired his work discipline.

"Okay, I hate to see you go." she added in a phony, syrupy voice, "But I'll be anxiously waiting your return. Bye for now."

"I'll bet you will." Dan mumbled as he returned the phone to it's cradle.

Dan went out to the porch, sat in the rocker, hoping he could still do it. He wished himself back to his own world.

He watched the pigeons pecking at crumbs in front of his favorite park bench. He looked around at what he knew as normal, smiled and headed for his office and studio.

Dan felt a sense of calm and relief come over him as he unlocked his office door. He made some coffee and settled himself behind his desk reclining his chair and hoisting his feet up to the desk. His mind was already in gear. The thought of the grass always being greener made him laugh. I guess I don't have it too bad here.

Lifting himself out of his funky state he reviewed his work calender and resigned himself to getting back to what he did best. The next few days flew by with only intermittent thoughts of the other world. Lunch time he spent in his office not wanting to see Ian again. Not just yet anyway. Almost a week went by before he gave any serious thought to *"That other world."* His work was totally caught up and he had booked nothing new. His week now over he packed a few things and pointed his car north. A few days in his friends cabin in the woods was just the right prescription for his restless mind.

Chapter 9

The cabin and it's surrounds truly was just what the doctor ordered. He had stopped at a store and purchased a few days supply of food and beer. He honestly planned to relax and clear his mind and hoped the challenge of the lake fish would help accomplish this.

Dan actually slept well this first night away. Up with the sun Dan gathered up his fishing gear and happily approached the lake. A small feeder stream caught his attention reminding him of the babbling brook he saw on the other world.

"So much for clearing the mind." he said aloud as his thoughts of the other world attacked from all directions. Finding a comfortable spot with his back against a tree Dan resigned himself to try and sort out his doubts and suspicions of this other Earth. Why was he so untrusting ? Now that he met Josh he knew he was not alone in his mistrust. He was also sure that there were probably others but reprisal fear kept them quiet. "What's behind this and why ?" Dan asked talking to no one but the trees and lake. Even more importantly, who is behind all this and why ?"

Dan had to laugh at himself. Not only was he talking to himself but he was now answering himself.

He watched the water lapping at the rocks of the lake edge and thought about the beginning of this whole mess.

"That's it." he said quite loud this time. "Why not start thinking of how this whole thing started. Maybe I can retrace this whole matter or do away with it. That would be even better yet." He thought of Ian and his park bench. This whole mess started with Ian. Ian seemed to be capable of reading his mind. "What else is Ian capable of I wonder ?" Dan said aloud again. "And why did I end up where I did ? I don't even know what state I was in. Could that placement have been controlled by Ian ? Josh did say he thought they were recruiting. Recruiting for what ? Why can't I travel once I'm there ? What is their secret ? And why a secret ?"

Dan shook his head vigorously to stop the rush of thoughts. He knew he wanted time to think the whole thing through but not want to do it in two minutes. He laughed at himself for allowing the onslaught of confusion.

"**O**ne step at a time." he counseled himself. He tossed a stone into the lake and watched hypnotically as the ripples fan out until they disappeared.

"*Now to get back to Ian.*" he thought readying his fishing pole. This whole "Other Planet" deal originated with Ian. Now I'm wondering if he has any control of this transference or is it something I have really accomplished by myself. If it is something I can accomplish by myself why did I end up where I did ?

Note to self, "The next time I will try to put myself someplace else. Second question, for now anyway, If it is an actual alternate universe, why are there so many restraints and who is controlling. Thinking again of Josh's remark about suspected recruiting, why would you do that if it truly was an alternate world. Why wouldn't everything be the same? Why recruit only certain people ? What is the end to these means ? If living there is being free of the rat race, having restrictions certainly does not accomplish that. Perhaps back here in my own real world is not such a bad thing after all. If I don't like my particular rat race I have the option of changing it. It is still my choice. So why am I considering another life.

Now that Dan just about talked himself out of transferring to another world he felt he still had to satisfy his curiosity about what was going on. Who knows maybe he could even help Josh get free. Also who knows how many others are stuck there.

Speaking out loud again; "That being decided let's see if I can catch dinner."

The thought of helping Josh get free intrigued Dan, but the how remained a mystery. Obviously, based on what he said that he was being watched, as was Dan, yet not to that degree as of the present moment. If he was free to go back and forth then why not Josh. Hence the control factor.

"I'm sure," thought Dan, *"if he was able to go back he most likely would not return, which again brings forth the question of why are people being held here ? For what reason are there restrictions as to movement ? You can travel but only with permission. Permission from whom ? Why do I need permission, and who is the one that controls and most importantly is the why behind it ? What is there to gain and now needs to be held ?"*

Dan shook his head, hopefully to clear it a little.

"Now getting back to helping Josh get free," Dan said aloud, "What if there are others stuck here. Forget that for now." he told himself, let's see how successful I am with me first.

Dan's head by now was a whirlwind of too many questions and a definite lack of answers.

Dan lost himself for a short while in the ripples in the water, intrigued by the bugs causing them. He could even see the fish slowly meandering with the flow of the fast current. This simple scene snapped his mind back to his problems.

"Why is there another world ? What's wrong with this one ? Whatever problems we may have we created ourselves. Is there really another world or is it only in my mind because I want it to be. ?" Dan's mind was going wild again. "Perhaps this man Ian is capable of putting thoughts into other minds as a sort of game he plays ?"

Dan gazed at the water again but continued his questions.

"If there is another world why is it such a secret ? If there is a duplicate planet then astronomers would know about it. I don't recall ever hearing of such a thing. So perhaps it is a mind game, though I must say it seems very real. Even as a mind game what is the purpose ? What will the end result be ?"

Enough with the questions Dan, you have been getting nowhere on a fast track. You should try working on something factual. Dan stopped himself there.

"That's it! Maybe that's exactly the answer I've been looking for and just didn't see it. Facts don't lie. They don't distort the brain. That's all well and good I thought but just where do I get the facts. Dan paused here again, his mind blank. Suddenly the light bulb came on. The Library. Of course stupid, that's what libraries are for. I'll check the public library and if need be the local college library.

He already began to feel better. "I'll take whatever time necessary before going back to the other world."

Dan, left the soothing water, packed up everything in a hurry and made straight for home and a good night's rest.

Chapter 10

Early the next morning found Dan sitting quietly in a corner of the local library almost hidden by a stack of books on the table before him. He chose three particular books after checking their indices for parallel universes, worlds, multiple universes. He soon found out that most of them said the same thing in different ways. The main fact being parallel worlds, universes, or what ever you wanted to call them, are possible. The experts go into all kinds of detail of Quantum Physics and probability factors but in the end all the answers come out the same. Parallel worlds are possible. The probability of this occurring in one's lifetime or even in our galaxies lifetime are extremely minute, nevertheless it was still possible.

Now Dan was really confused. He did and did not want to believe. The quantum explanation was dealing with electrons. Something the human eye can't even see yet Dan was a flesh and blood six foot human being who was actually living the experience. Something was not coming together in his head.

After inquiry, Dan was notified he could not check any of these reference books out for further study. So the next hour was taken up with getting copies of the pages he thought pertinent. He eventually matched them with a book title and author just for future reference.

The main theme that actually caught his attention was from the book entitled "Parallel Worlds" by Michio Kaku. "The passage Dan was riveted on stated,

"Being a Quantum Theory, Particle Physics states that there is a finite probability for unlikely events to occur, such as the creation of parallel universes."

Just about all the other books he reviewed said the same thing in a variety of ways. As far fetched as this was, it was real. He was sure it was real because he was living it. Or was he ?

The thought of the mind game reentered his thinking. He felt it could not be ruled out. Dan sat back in the chair, closed his eyes and let his mind wander.

"Sir! Are you finished with these books ? We're closing soon.

The librarian was super polite but you could see she was anxious to be on her way. Dan smiled himself back to reality and finally replied;

"Not to worry, Mam, I'll return these books to where they belong and be out of here in a jiffy. He counted the copy pages he made, turned over a five dollar bill and bid a pleasant day to the patient librarian.

As he walked home he thought, *"Thank goodness for big city libraries and the readily available selection of such books that would not be easily accessible in smaller libraries."*

Dan made his way back to his apartment avoiding the park altogether. "I desperately needed some alone time, I had to think, to think as clearly and uninterrupted as possible." Dan thought speaking to himself out loud.

Once home he locked the door, disconnected the phone and made some coffee. He settled himself down with his fresh brewed coffee and gazed at the wispy clouds he could see out his window. For a while his mind just went blank. Dan had no idea how long his head was in limbo but when he did return to the real world he was somewhat refreshed.

He refilled his coffee mug which had grown cold during his brain drain.

His mind, again engaged in thought. Laughing to himself he reviewed what he had just learned. Speaking aloud "Now that I have all this information, what good is it unless I can apply it. I can't apply it because I don't know how. Quantum Physics is one thing which I really know nothing about, and the physical reality I'm dealing with is another. Or is this all a mental thing I'm going through or perhaps being subconsciously put through by my park bench associate."

Chapter 11

Having had no success the night before in finding an answer to his dilemma he awoke in a working mood and decided to go to his studio and lose himself on some darkroom work. He chose some older glamor model negatives to work on in hopes they would help refocus his mind on more tangible things.

Deeply involved with his retouching pencils he almost did not hear the buzzer indicating someone entering the waiting room slash sales room. Cursing himself for forgetting to lock the door he left the dimly lighted work room squinting his eyes against the lighting of the waiting room.

"Hi Uncle Dan. Mom said I could visit with you while she does some shopping."

"Oh, lucky me." Dan thought. *"Just what I need, a talks too much*

twelve year old."

"Hi, Billy." Dan said putting on a phony smile. He walked to the door and turned the lock to keep out any further intrusions.

"How come you're locking the door ?"

"Well, I really don't have any appointments today so I thought I would catch up on some darkroom work."

*"Why am I explaining to a twelve year old."*he thought

"Don't let me stop you Unk, I'll just watch." replied the youngster as he followed Dan to the small darkened room.

"Wow ! She's pretty. Bill remarked.

"Yes she is and now if you don't mind I have some work to finish up."

"Okay, sorry Unk, I'll try to be quiet."

Billy wandered through the room looking at all the pictures while Dan tried to focus on his retouching. The silence lasted for about eight minutes before Billy started in again.

"Wow ! That's a great picture of the moon, Unk. When did you take that ? It looks like you were right on top of it. Look at all them craters. I just saw a movie that had a picture of the moon just like that, but not as good as yours."

Dan was about ready to tell the boy to shut up when Billy continued.

"The story was about this guy who went to another universe or a different world but just like ours. They said something about a parallel universe."

This immediately caught Dan's attention.

"Oh really." Dan remarked not wanting to sound too anxious. "And how did this guy get to this other world ?"

I don't exactly know." was Billy's answer. "They talked about a lot of stuff I didn't understand."

"Like what for instance ?" Dan inquired.

"Something like quality or quantity physics and such."

"You mean Quantum Physics ?"

"Yeah ! That was it, Quanta--, what ever you said, and a lot of other stuff like electrons and phototons and junk. They even talked about time travel through worm holes in space. It's bad enough we got worms in our garden and now we got worms in space." I guess that's why they call it science fiction."

Dan was holding back his laughter now for he did not want to embarrass the boy. "So." he thought, "They were basing their movie on the same kind of research he had done himself."

"Tell me more about this movie Billy. Did you like it ?"

"Yeah, I guess." he answered. "I think it was pretty silly though, having two planets exactly alike."

"How did it end ?" Dan further pushed.

"I don't know exactly." was again Billy's answer. "The hero or star of the movie figured out some kind of mathematical formula that sent him back to his world. It didn't say how though, or even if they did I didn't understand it."

"What was the name of the movie." Dan asked directly.

"That was the other funny thing." Billy replied excitedly. "It was called "The Other Planet Earth"

Dan did not want to push this too much further so he ended the conversation with "Sounds interesting, I'll have to try and rent it sometime."

"I think they may have it in RED Box." was Billy's reply.

"Okay thanks for the information, but right now I have to finish this retouching."

"Okay, sorry Unk, I didn't mean to disturb you."

Both uncle and nephew became silent, Dan with his retouching and Billy looking through photo albums and magazines.

An hour and a half passed when Billy broke the silence.

"Wow, look at the time, I promised Mom I would meet her downstairs about now. So long Uncle Dan, it was fun being here, see ya."

The door closed behind him and all was quiet again.

Dan thought about his nephew, he wasn't a bad kid, funny at times, but under the present circumstances he purely did not have the interest to interact with him properly.

Dan put aside the retouching and sat at the table that doubled as his desk. Reaching for a writing tablet and pencil he thought if he started to list all the incidents that took place so far he could then make himself a more unobstructed picture, and assist him in finding an answer to this confusion. He reviewed in his mind every detail he could recall to date and recorded it in the most accurate way possible.

With three pages finished, Dan sat back to review what he had just written. He read it carefully, three times making a few corrections and additions. The pattern was all the same. His travel to and from the other earth was all basically physical. He did not know how it was done. He just knew that he was physically moved from one place to the other.

Putting all that aside he turned to the library research notes. Dan read and reread all the pages he highlighted from the countless books he scanned. Apparently the possibility exists of duplicate worlds, according to quantum physics, but actual performance of such a feat was yet untested. Even the theoretical ability seemed limited to sub atomic particles. The math was there but the observation of its results was yet to be fulfilled.

Dan felt even more frustrated, and the problem, still unsolved in his head, was pushed to the side while he rearranged his negative files with almost robotic moves.

Having no idea of the time, he decided he needed a change of scenery. Outside the sun was shining in a cloudless sky. He felt a pull to his park bench and willfully proceeded in the opposite direction. Ian was the last person he wanted to see until he had some answers. Aimlessly wandering the city streets he started thinking of the quiet country road in the other world. And suddenly found himself there. Looking around confused he saw he was alone.

"**N**ow how did that happen." He asked himself out loud. There was no answer for which he was almost thankful. He stopped to gaze at the beautiful country view thinking how different it was from the city crowd he just left.

He felt the pressing of people to be confining and realized he was back in the city. He was standing still in the mass of moving people. The pressure he was feeling was real. It was obviously annoying people trying to navigate around him accompanied by a few disgruntled comments. Dan finally moved steering his way to his apartment.

Once safely inside he sat down cradling his head in his hands. He sat this way for sometime, thinking of absolutely nothing, his mind an involuntary blank. The whine of an ambulance siren passing on the street below disturbed this unasked for trance. Dan then realized he actually felt better.

"**W**hy do I do this to myself, this self imposed worry and concern." He said talking out loud to no one. "Over what ? Off on a momentary tangent from norm ? I could ignore this temporary disruption of my routine and live happily ever after. Let's face it, if this pressure of deadlines was too much to live with I could move to a small town anywhere. That was one of the great advantages of my profession. I could set up anywhere."

Dan was laughing now.

"You silly idiot, you're doing it again."

Regaining his composure he resolved to apply some logical thought, at least as close to it as he could come.

"Physics says its possible. Logic tells me it's not. I could forget the whole thing and go on with my life as usual. Then again if it is real, what about the others trapped in another world they can not escape from."

Dan often argued with himself but never on something this crucial. That thought made up his mind. He has to get to the bottom of this. Walking to the kitchen, he closed his mind temporarily , to the nagging problem and decided some food was in order. There was not much of a selection but it would do.

Reviewing his work schedule he concluded nothing was pressing so made up his mind to make another visit to this mysterious other dimension, or planet or universe, or whatever else it may be called. When there he would make every effort possible to see Josh again. Dan wanted to share his latest physics discoveries regarding worlds and at the same time collect whatever new information Josh may have come across. Tomorrow early sounded okay to Dan. He would try to place himself on the quiet road outside of town and then walk to his cabin motel and try his luck at a rendevous with Josh.

Not wanting to go near the park because of Ian, he decided to transport from his apartment. He made himself comfortable and let his mind move to the country road.

~ ~ ~ ~

Dan followed the road toward the motel. He was glad there was no one else on the road. He really did not want any diversions right now. He picked up his pace going through town hoping to avoid others. As he passed the coffee shop the woman who ran it waved hello with a warm welcome back smile. Dan returned a quick nod of his head and continued towards his destination. He did not want any interruptions at this point, nor did he want any sort of distractions that might dissuade him from his mission of truth seeking.

He managed to get through to the motel at the far end of town without incident although he did notice a different air about town. The people he did see appeared to be more reserved than usual. Quiet and reserved as if something serious or tragic had occurred.

Dan reaching the office of the motel area only to find a new face greeting him.

"Welcome back Mr. Morgan, and how long will you be with us this visit ?"

"Just a few days." Dan lied, "I still have business affairs to clean up. I don't want to leave anything undone."

"I quite agree with that work ethic. To bad all people didn't think that way."

Dan detected a shallowness to his words. Something he was witness to quite often on his visits here. Trying not to create any suspicions he added;

"Josh taking the day off ?"

"More than just the day I'm afraid. He's no longer with us." Catching himself he continued with, "He decided to visit other parts of this new world. He even mentioned he would be gone for an indefinite period of time."

Dan playing along with the charade replied;

"Well I wish him luck, he seemed like a nice guy. And your name ?"

"Oh, please forgive my manners, my name is Travis, Travis

Donaldson. I'll be your host here until they get someone permanently."

"Well, if that end cabin is still available, I think I'll just settle down for the day."

"Yes Sir, Mr. Morgan, it's just as you left it, here's the key and I'll leave you undisturbed."

"Thanks much, Travis, I guess I'll see you later then. Nice meeting you."

Dan took the key and slowly walked to the cabin. Once inside he felt he could think normal again. He felt bad about Josh knowing how he wanted to get away. He recalled how nervous he was the night they met in his room and how he said he was being watched. Dan wondered now if he was being watched also because of his connection with Josh. The easy thing to do would be to go back to his original world and forget everything. Dan just could not do that. There was something not right going on here and he wanted to get to the bottom of it before they eliminated him also.

There had to be someone else like Josh who questioned this too perfect a world. The problem was how does one go about finding that person. Apparently everybody watched everybody else. This is like the stories you hear about the cold war in the fifties and early sixties, thought Dan.

Dan thought of Daria again. She seemed to be in the know but obviously not completely. Should he try to cozy up to her to see what she may reveal, if anything. Right now that seemed like his only option. He knew he could not trust her but perhaps if he played totally dumb he could pick up some useful information. Dan finally convinced himself this was his best way to go. Now the only thing left for him to do was to find Daria. Remembering it was nearing lunchtime he headed back to town and the café. That would be as good a place to start as any. The woman that ran the café saw Dan from the window and was enthusiastically waving as if she were expecting him. She greeted Dan with a warm hug whispering;

"**J**osh said you would be back. I'll talk to you later."

Dan immediately picked up on her warning and acted like a long lost friend.

"**I** thought I might find Daria here today." he said.

The relief in her eyes was proof, to him anyway, of her sincerity. Dan did not give any sign of her secret.

Now talking openly she said;

Daria, oh yes Daria. I saw her day before yesterday, let's see I believe she said she would be in today sometime after one PM. Can I get you some lunch, that is if you want to wait."

Dan played along for appearances sake. "I'd like to see the menu though. I'm not sure what I want."

She smiled, acting normal. "Comin right up." Returning with the menu she added, "Today's soup special is Potato Leek." and went to help another customer. Dan put in his food order with both he and the woman acting totally normal as waitress and customer. When Dan was almost finished eating the check was given. Without notice of anyone else she managed to indicate two checks. One, the actual itemized food list, the second a hand written note Dan successfully secreted it away while reaching for his wallet.

Dan just finished paying the bill when Daria entered. A slight disturbance showed on her face and in her eyes which she quickly recovered from. Putting on her usual happy so glad you're here smile she walked directly to Dan.

"I'm so glad you're back. Get all your affairs straightened out ?" She asked in a syrupy voice.

"Not quite, but almost." he answered.

This answer appeared to please Daria. Dan noticed this also.

Perhaps, he thought, she will be more relaxed with him. *"I will play with that angle some more and hopefully get her to open up some."*

"I'm glad I ran into you again, I thought maybe we could do a dinner again, but not too late. The last couple of days at work were pretty rough. I really need to get some rest and what better place to do that then here in Peaceful Valley."

Dan was warmly smiling through this whole discourse. From the look on Daria's face his plan was working. He felt she was believing his story.

"I guess I could make myself free this evening though I do have an appointment this afternoon. Let's say I pick you up at around four forty five. We'll go to the same restaurant. I really like the food there."

"Four forty five it is. That will give me time to shower and clean up. I'm so looking forward to dinner with you."

Reading her body language and facial expression Dan felt confident that Daria bought his innocent act. Thinking to himself again, *"Now to see if I can carry this off for the rest of the night."*

As Dan left the café he said good bye to the owner waitress like any other customer making it a point to catch a quick glimpse at her name tag, Eleanor. She smiled politely returning a good bye and gave Dan a cautious wink, imperceptible to anyone else.

Outside and walking back to his cabin he remembered the note but chose not to read it until he was in the privacy of his room.

Safely out of sight of others Dan retrieved the note from his pocket.

"Dan, please be on your guard. There are those here who do not want you free thinking. I'll explain more tonight after midnight."

"Wow ! Thought Dan. "That's a powerful mouth full. It sort of fits in with my misgivings of this whole affair. I could go home now and forget forever that this ever existed."

But down deep inside Dan knew he could not do that and leave others stuck here against their will.

"What is behind this all, and more importantly why ?"

Dan stood confused, looking out the window at nothing in particular.

Shaking off this confused mind set he proceeded to shower and shave and get ready for his evening with Daria. She arrived exactly on time, not a minute sooner or later. Dan was barely in the car when Daria took off. Seeing his reaction she excused herself;

"I made reservations, I don't want to be late."

Dan laughed internally. *"The last time we were there, there were more empty tables than people."*

The conversation on the ride to the restaurant was the usual generalities, weather etc.

"She's playing it cool again." he thought. Dan went along with her mood.

The restaurant was as he figured, about a third full. Looking around Dan could swear they were the same people that were here last time. He acted as if he didn't notice, but cautioned himself to be careful. Smiling, he told Daria how lovely she looked this evening. He must have caught her unaware because he thought he detected an actual blush cross her face. They even had a glass of wine while waiting for their dinner order.

"I assume you still have questions and perhaps I can help you." Daria said getting straight to the point.

"As a matter of fact I do." Dan replied in a happy tone to keep Daria off guard.

"I'm still a little confused about money. Do I bring it all with me? Suppose after a year or so I decided I wanted to go back. I would need money when I returned there. What is the usual procedure ? Dan picked up on a look of relief in her face.

"That, of course, has an easy answer," Daria replied. "Leave some in a savings account. No checking, savings only. That way not too much notice is given about no transactions for over a year. You need not worry about that though, because if you stay here for a year you wont be__"

Here she caught herself. " You wont want to go back. That's the beauty of this place. A very contagious atmosphere of relaxation with no hustle and bustle."

Dan caught the slip but did not physically react.

"You're right, that was an easy answer."

"Okay, next question ?" she asked even more relaxed than before."

"I know we discussed this before, I believe it was the time with what's his name, Ted, I think. About travel. Believe it or not I forgot what you and he said. I'm interested in going to France. In speaking with other photographers I understand the towns and countryside are just begging to be photographed."

Dan said this with enthusiasm to put his point across.

"I believe we said it would be okay as long as you had permission, you know, passport and travel papers."

"She slipped again with that permission stuff." thought Dan. As he sipped his wine and glanced at Daria over the rim of the glass he detected an uneasiness.

"If you would please excuse me." she said all warm and schmoozy, "I need to go to the powder room."

"Of course." Dan smiled back.

She left the table as he busied himself refilling both their wine glasses. Dan, following her with his eyes, trying not to be obvious, saw her stop at a back table just before the hallway to the rest rooms. She chatted a minute or so prior to entering the ladies room. It was a man, his back to Dan. For whatever reason there was a familiarity about the head. As Daria passed the table he turned his head enough for Dan to see it was- - - - yes it was Ian.

Questions filled his mind. "Why is he here ? Why is Daria talking to him on the sly ? Why is he being secretive ?

Daria returned to the table all smiles and more at ease.

"I was doing some more thinking about your question. I don't think there will be any trouble with you visiting France, with a passport of course."

"So she got permission from the boss, did she." thought Dan. *"That just confirms, for me anyway, that something is not right. Let me just throw her a tidbit to keep her guessing."*

"Would you allow me another question ?"

"Of course Dan, anything you want." Daria answered full of smiles.

"What about housing?" asked Dan much to Daria's pleasure.

"Do you buy, rent, build ?" Dan figured this would keep her off guard, thinking he was really going to stay.

All bubbly and happy now, Daria replied willingly.

"You can have any of the above Dan."

"I must have really gotten to her." thought Dan. *"That's the first time she ever used his name."*

"And if not in this community, there are a few neighboring villages that are absolutely lovely."

"That sounds great, I guess I'll have to start checking them out." answered Dan.

"Well, if you would like I would be more than willing to go with you. You know, the woman's point of view." volunteered Daria, almost too exuberantly

"I'll keep that in mind." Dan smiled back.

The rest of the evening was normal chit chat of no consequence with Daria bubbling all night.

Dan was back at the Worry Free Motel a little after nine. He did not invite Daria in though the signs were there that she was waiting for the opportunity.

Finally alone again Dan turned the lights on in his little cabin. He checked outside a few times to see if he was being watched. Trying to play it normal he turned the lights out one by one over a period of time. Around eleven the last light went off. He left the door unlocked and even checked outside again after about ten minutes. Everything appeared to be clear. Some stars were visible and there was a half moon which provided enough light to see the area around the cabin. Dan retreated into the cabin again and made himself as comfortable as possible, considering how tense he felt.

Three minutes after midnight there was a light tap on the door. Dan opened it slowly and was taken by surprise as a pair of warm arms enfolded him and sweet tasting lips joined his in a lingering kiss. He could tell by the perfume it was Eleanor and returned the kiss and embrace with a feeling he had not felt in a long time. His surprise lover at last broke the kiss whispering;

"That should convince anyone that is watching what our intentions are. Dan started to move back inside the cabin when Eleanor stopped him.

"No let's walk by the water for a while. I don't trust that the rooms aren't bugged. It's been known to happen. And thanks for the kiss, I didn't know how you were going to react."

"Did I pass the test ?" Dan asked.

"With flying colors and then some. I have to admit, you made me feel like a woman again."

"My pleasure Mam and I really mean that.

Eleanor grasped his hand and gave it a warm squeeze.

"I don't know where to start." Dan said hesitantly.

"Then let me start for you." interrupted Eleanor. "Josh told me about you."

Dan took on a cautious look.

Eleanor took note of his caution right away.

"Relax Dan, I'm on your side. As I said, Josh told me all about you. He said you could be trusted. I know all about your midnight meeting with him, hence the kiss. They were on to Josh, I'm guessing for some time, because it wasn't long after you went back that he went on vacation."

"In other words." Dan filled in. "He disappeared."

"You got it." said Eleanor firmly. "Josh and I had worked together for some time, trying to figure out what this place really is. There are a few others who have joined us. I don't think they have suspected me as of yet, but who knows after tonight."

"I'm so sorry." Dan said protectively. "I didn't mean to put you in jeopardy."

"Not to worry Dan. I want to be here." Again she squeezed his hand warmly.

Dan collecting his thoughts asked straight on;

"Who is or are "They" He emphasized the they.

"That my friend is the sixty four thousand dollar question. We were sure of some of the underlings but not a clue of the top people or even why. The concept of another world, a peaceful world, was intriguing to all of us. Obviously that's why we're here. Now it seems we're stuck here against our will."

"But I though we could come and go at our pleasure." commented

Dan.

"Ah yes, that was the biggest piece of bait they use. Are you here because of Ian ?"

"As a matter of fact, yes."

"And he seems to be able to get inside your head, am I correct."

"Yes." Dan answered sheepishly.

"Don't feel bad." Eleanor said in a comforting voice. "We were all caught that way. Most went on to be satisfied, I guess. A few of us questioned the paradise too often. Josh being one who was very vocal and insisted on answers."

"Hence, his disappearance." Dan added again. "So you have no idea who or what is behind whatever ?"

"As crazy as that sounds that is essentially correct. Every time we think we have a lead, we really have nothing."

Dan was quiet trying to think. Eleanor pushed closer to him making sure his arms encircled her as she lay her head on his chest. Dan did not push her away.

"Can you go back ?" he asked Eleanor.

"Perhaps one more time, but I know Ian would be right there. Josh and I figured out that if we decided not to return to this world we would probibly disappear from our original world also."

'So that's why I saw Ian the other night. I was being watched.' "Dan thought.

"**H**as any sort of plan of escape been developed ?" inquired Dan holding Eleanor a little more snugly.

Josh was working on something. He even said he had written certain instructions for all of us." answered Eleanor.

"**W**here are these instructions ?"

"**G**ood question. Josh indicated he would show us all as soon as you returned. I assumed he had plans for you also."

"**H**e may have but he never disclosed anything about such plans." Dan explained.

A sudden chill ran through Eleanor as she looked up at Dan, fear tinting her face.

"**I**f they were found then we could all be in serious danger." she said.

"**I** don't think you have to worry about that." Dan stated reassuringly. "If they were found you wouldn't be here with me now."

He leaned down and kissed her gently. She did not pull away.

"What was that for." she asked quietly.

"Just for show." Dan answered quickly, then talking more softly, "Besides I wanted to."

"I'm glad." she answered as she snuggled deeper into his arms. They remained in the quiet embrace for a while with Dan finally breaking the mood.

"If there were instructions, then we'll have to find them." he said this with authority. "Do you know the others involved with you and Josh ?"

"No, for security reasons each of us only knows of one other person." Eleanor answered.

"Good idea." mumbled Dan obviously thinking of the next step. "Give me another day to search for these papers and if I can't find them I'll come up with my own plan. In the meantime get in touch with your contact to pass this information on but be on the lookout for any hint whatsoever of a "Who or Why"

Eleanor feeling better with Dan's confidence looked up at him smiling;

"Yes Sir, Boss."

Dan laughed softly and kissed her forehead.

"Now young lady you had better be going. You have to work tomorrow."

"Aren't you going to ask me in." she purred softly.

"No, I am not. We both have a lot to do and I need a clear head to do it. With you around my head certainly will not be clear."

"You're no fun." she pouted as they walked back to the road. Before they parted Dan held her arms firmly and looking directly into her eyes;

"I'm going to take you out of here, I promise."

With that he kissed her lightly, turned and walked to his cabin.

Eleanor remained frozen in place as she watched Dan until he was inside his cabin. She slowly walked down the road feeling loved but confused.

Chapter 12

Dan felt sorry for both he and Eleanor but he did need a clear head.

He knew no more now than yesterday but was more determined than ever to get to the bottom of this mystery. Not just for his own sake but for countless others to come. He wished he could also help those of the past. He lay down, clothes and all still feeling Eleanor's warmth. He knew he wanted to be up with the sun and set his watch alarm accordingly.

Confidence within him, Dan was truly up with the sun. He started searching the cabin for hiding places for Josh's plans. He was going by instinct and his told him Josh did not hide them in his office or cabin. He had strong feelings that they were hidden here where he was staying. He methodically went through the cabin's every nook and cranny, checking for loose boards and all from ceiling to floor. Every piece of furniture was viewed inside and out. It was eight-ish when he finished inside the cabin.

Dan sat down at the table to think and immediately jumped up again.

"**T**he night he came to visit." he said aloud, then looked around to make sure no was listening. He smiled to himself. Now just thinking he continued his one person conversation.

*"**T**he night he came to visit I got the hint he may have been outside for a time before he knocked on the door. Do I dare look around in the daylight ? Perhaps I should wait until dark. Now what do I do with myself all day."*

He thought briefly of Eleanor than rejected the idea for two reasons. First she was working and second he still needed that clear head.

While having coffee he remembered seeing a watering can outside by the entrance steps. That might be the very thing he thought, to allow him to look outside the cabin without drawing attention. There were some lovely flowers growing in front of each unit, his included. Why not get in good with the environment.

Pleased with himself Dan finished his coffee and went outside as if it were a normal day. He checked the flower beds and they really did need water. He checked areas of the cabin as he reached for the water can. He continued checking as he watered.

"Hi there ." Dan heard from behind. It was Travis.

"Thank goodness I wasn't checking the cabin at that point." thought Dan.

"Good morning." he returned pleasantly.

"We have people to do that you know." Travis commented.

"I figured as much." Dan answered, "But they seemed a little droopy, so I thought I could give them a helping hand. I don't have anything else planned, though I might do a little fishing later."

"It's a great day for it." Travis replied. "Well good luck with your angling." and strode away whistling.

"That was close Dan said out loud to himself while he waited for Travis to disappear.

Dan had no luck with the obvious hiding places on the outside of the cabin. He finished the watering chore and was returning to the door steps when he noticed a board on the second step was loose. He sat on the top step as if resting and played with the loose step. Slowly he was able to move it enough to see the darkness of a cavity beneath. He sat back resting and to make sure he was not observed. With an extra effort he was able to pry the step completely off allowing the sun to illuminate the inside. His head spinning and heart thumping a bit faster he leaned forward to see absolutely nothing. Disappointment shot through his whole being. He recovered seconds later and as usual scolded himself.

"*What did you expect, stupid. That's what you get for letting your imagination control your common sense. Josh was too alert to do such a foolish thing. The papers will have to wait for another time..*"

Dan replaced the step as best he could and told himself to notify Travis the next time he saw him.

Dan strolled to the stream, fishing gear in tow. He actually did not plan on fishing, the gear was just for looks. Trying to be analytical, he listed some facts, softly speaking out loud.

"Okay, what do we have that's positive. Number one, Josh disappeared. Two, there is already an underground in place. Three, there was a thought out plan, but the papers have disappeared. Four, I can still travel back and forth but who knows for how long. Five, I promised Eleanor I would get her out of here and who knows how many others. Not much in the way of pluses weighed against all the negative.

Now for a plan. Ha! That's as far as I get. Think positive Dan," he said letting the water take his mind downstream.

"That's it." he shouted. He looked around and assured himself he was alone. "Positive thinking." he continued. "If one person can think his or her way to a parallel world, why wouldn't a group mind set be able to do the same thing. All concentrating on the same place."

Dan rolled this thought around a while, not having any prior experience into Tele-Portation, if that is what it is.

"I remember reading something about group positive thinking." he resumed his conversation with himself. "Of course there were a lot of pro's and con's involved but if I recall correctly the pro's won out. Naturally there would be the need for extreme commitment to this. I wonder just how many people there are in this rebel group."

Dan was actually beginning to like this idea of being a rebel. It was like fulfilling a need that he harbored for a long time.

"Okay, so number one on my list is to find out how many people we're talking about who want to leave. Based on that number we must find a place for all to meet that will be safe. The plan can not be released until the last minute, for secrecy reasons, obviously."

Dan felt good about his thoughts, so good that he actually started to fish. If he was being watched he was totally innocent. He rested his back against a tree and made up his mind to have a late lunch / early dinner at the café' in town, not that Eleanor had anything to do with that decision.

Deciding he had killed enough time to make it look good, Dan retrieved his fishing gear and strolled back to his room. He washed away the days dirt and took off for the café'.

Eleanor was obviously glad to see him as evidenced by the flush on her face. They both played it friendly but no more than cook and patron.

With Eleanor's many visits to his booth by the window Dan was able to get his message across. Dan could sense the disappointment in Eleanor when he said he was leaving again to go back to his original home for a couple of days. She understood the necessity of his leaving but that did not take away the emptiness she felt.

"I will adhere to your instructions starting tonight so that by your return the first step will be complete." she managed to whisper.

In paying his dinner tab Eleanor managed a lingering touch of his hand that had a clear meaning to both of them.

~ ~ ~ ~

~ ~ ~ ~

Once out in the fresh air and sunshine Dan turned in the opposite direction from his temporary cabin. Making sure he was alone his thoughts focused on his park bench and before he was even aware he was watching the pigeons at his feet.

"Thank goodness Ian is not here." he said aloud and hurried back to his office to avoid the possibility of his presence.

Safely locked in his office, he had time to think.

"First things first." Dan spoke out loud. "I must get back to the library. There is something I must check out."

Topics such as Cosmology and Quantum Physics were not you everyday cup of tea in a small town. The big city does have its advantages.

Dan locked the studio and went straight to the library. Familiar with the section he wanted from the last visit he walked directly to it. Choosing half a dozen books he found a quiet corner table and started to digest the contents. Finding something he felt suited his needs he copied it down.

"Once we open the door to applying Quantum fluctuations to the universe, we are almost forced to admit the possibility of parallel universes."

Further reading netted more results.

"To slip between these parallel worlds is within the laws of physics."

Pleased with himself, Dan read on and again found something he thought pertinent.

"Intelligent beings may be able to travel between quantum realities."

His mind was working overtime and his eyes grew weary. He gladly welcomed the announcement the library was closing. Returning the reference material to its proper shelf , he left for his apartment making sure he was not followed.

"I hope I'm not being too paranoid." he thought.

Once safely home he thawed out a frozen pizza and that was his late supper along with a cold beer. His mind went right to work.

"If all these things are possible according to Quantum Theories, and if life is out there from other universes and planets, and perhaps they are more advanced than we are, we could be a parallel world to them. Therefore they can be traveling to this world, to my world. Ian perhaps ? Ian and others."

"Whoa, boy." Dan cautioned himself. "Where are you going with all this. There is no proof of what you just put forth, this is just your own imaginings, and weird at that, even for you. But," he continued to argue with himself. "There is also no proof that it can't exist."

He let these things settle in his mind while he went to the fridge for another beer. Repositioned in another chair Dan's mind opened another chapter.

"Why have I taken this upon myself. I could just as easily not go back at all and resign myself to stay in the rat race.."

He was quick to answer himself.

"I took this upon myself because it is the right thing to do. There are obviously many others caught in between that can't help themselves.

Right now I will have to go with my own thoughts that my present world is the right one."

Dan paused and reached for the TV remote, clicked it on and within seconds turned it off.

"I'm enough of my own distraction." he said aloud.

"I need a plan. That's a brilliant statement of the obvious

you Idiot."

He recalled reading in one of those books about "Balance" and "Harmony" to paraphrase what he read.

"I should probably take notes so I remember the proper terminology. Wait a minute Dummy, you did take notes." Dan scolded himself again. "I'm beginning to believe I'm my own worst critic."

He found some notes folded up in his wallet.

"Perhaps this will help." he thought as he read the first note.

"Being a Quantum theory, particle physics states that there is a finite probability for unlikely events to occur, such as the creation of parallel universes"

Dan remembered reading this on his first trip to the library.

This was followed by;

"If electrons can exist in parallel states hovering between existence and nonexistence, then why can't the universe."

"A little over my head but I think I grasp the basic idea. Let's face it, it must be possible, I'm living it."

He flipped through another page.

"There are many anomalies that are an integral part of general relativity. The strangest of these is the possibility of parallel universes and gateways connecting them."

That fits in with my other note .

"To slip between these worlds is within the laws of physics."

"Now that, I know to be true. This next note follows true also."

"Intelligent beings may be able to travel between Quantum realities."

"Though my intelligence may be questionable by some." Dan chided himself.

Dan rested a moment trying to digest this, out of his league, mumbo jumbo. He then remembered a third paper. It took a few minutes to find but eventually he located it in his jacket pocket.

$\left(1\right)$ Wave functions are the same between worlds or can be different.

$\left(2\right)$ Any contamination from outside sources prevents this similarity and they cannot interact any more.

The final note on the bottom of the pile struck a note with him also.

"In the real world, objects interact with the environment, and the slightest interaction with the outside world can disturb the two wave functions, and then they start to "decohere", that is , fall out of synchronization and separate. Once the two wave functions are no longer vibrating with each other, the two wave functions no longer interact with each other."

"That's what I was looking for when I said "Balance"

Dan said almost shouting.

He sat back to calm himself down and reorganize his head.

"First of all a parallel universe or world is possible. Second, you can travel back and forth. Third, we are in balance, or in order to be more correct, the wave functions are the same. Fourth, wave contamination can prevent total interaction. Fifth, is? What is fifth? I don't know where I go from here."

Dan was stumped. He went to the kitchen, was going to get another beer but thought better of it. He needed to keep a clear head. He grabbed the orange juice instead. Returning to his notes, he covered them up, rather than be confused by them.

He let his mind drift back to his original thought. If more than one mind was concentrating on the same thing, we should be able to overpower whatever force is being used against us. *"I don't know why, but I feel confident it will work."* He told himself.

His thoughts then drifted back to the instructions he gave Eleanor. I don't know how many there are being unwillingly held but the more concentrating minds the better our chances, he laughingly convinced himself.. Now, if this works, what then ? How do we keep people like Ian from either trying to stop us or coming after us.

~ ~

Strange thoughts began nagging at Dan. At first he considered them ridiculous, yet the more he thought the less ridiculous they became. He knew traveling to an alternate world was a fact. What if these people from this other world were traveling here to take over, to replace us for who knows what reasons.

"Now you're really losing it Dan." he said aloud. "You have watched much too much Science Fiction as a kid."

Dan got up laughing at himself and returned his empty Orange juice glass to the sink without bothering to rinse it. Back to his notes and questions again.

"How do we shut this doorway once we have transported to home safe and sound ? The notes said contamination of the waves prevents travel between worlds. Oh great now I need a Quantum Physicist. Of course I'll just look one up in the phone book."

Feeling lost and at a dead end he stretched out on the sofa staring at the ceiling.

"Why is this haunting me so ? If Quantum Physics allows for the possibility of other worlds then why can some, and not all, move back and forth ?"

Dan remembered he still had some library books.

"Perhaps some more reading, what harm can it do."

He read non stop for about ten minutes. Suddenly "That's it." He yelled. "This may be my answer. He realized he was back to the balance and wave function again. Now new words jingled in his mind, Coherence and De-coherence.

"This has got to be my answer. It may not be proper procedure for Quantum Physics but it sounds logical to me."

Dan started writing his plan as he read.

"The two worlds have to be vibrating in perfect synchronization.

The slightest interaction or disturbance of the parallel wave function makes them de-cohere. Once they fall out of synchronization, travel between the two worlds ceases. So" he thought on, "If we disturb the wave function once all of us are have transported through we should break the connection. The other world will not cease to exist, but it will no longer be connected to this one I live on. It may go on to travel to other distant universes and find another compatible wave function and become a parallel world to it and allow travel between the two. I really don't care about that, at least I, or we, can live own lives again, rat race and all.

Dan paused here to let himself calm down. He closed his eyes and thought of Eleanor. This pleased him, which surprised him. He had never been in a serious relationship before and now he was looking forward to it.

Getting back to the more pressing problem;

"Now I need something of a significant disturbance to vibrate the atoms at our gateway.

"Since I am not a Quantum Physics expert, not even close to the words, I have only my purely layman's common sense to rely on. With my brain, my whole theory is probably down the drain." Dan berated himself.

I need to explode something. Something with enough power to disturb the atoms in the air."

Dan's mind momentarily went blank. He sat perfectly still looking at nothing in particular. A car backfired in the street below breaking the spell of mindlessness.

"That's it ! I still have some fireworks from July. Naaa, I'm sure that would not be powerful enough. What I need is a real explosive charge. Perhaps dynamite. That will never do, that creates other problems and questions. First of all dynamite is next to impossible to acquire, secondly, and more importantly, how do you explode it with out hurting someone, not to mention drawing a lot of unwanted attention."

Dan's spirits dipped a little again.

"I need some sort of explosion to distort the electron fabric of the area where we reenter this world, yet I have to make it as inconspicuous as possible. From what I read it won't take much but at the same time powerful enough to disturb atoms and electrons."

Now he was just confusing himself yet again. Taking a breather he went to the kitchen and made himself a cup of coffee. He still wanted to keep his head clear. He munched on a few stale cookies with the coffee.

No matter how hard Dan tried he could not think of anything to use except dynamite. He resigned himself to that fact and went on to think about acquiring at least one small stick. Even that was a problem. In today's political climate you need a damned good reason to purchase it. What do I tell them, "I want to blow up another planet from another universe." They will really take me away then.

He sat down and decided to face reality. The dynamite is out of the question. He went to his storage closet to check on the left over fire works. To his pleasant surprise he had more than he remembered. There were a couple of matts of twenty each and four M-80'S. With renewed enthusiasm he returned to the kitchen table with his box of goodies. Sitting staring at his treasure an idea popped out of nowhere. A timed fuse might just do what he was looking for. Patiently he dug through the box finding what he was looking for, long fuse material. For the next hour or so he lit and timed different lengths of fuse. He calculated that thirty seconds would be adequate Of course that also depended on how many people they end up with that want to go home, their real home. He could adjust the fuse length at the last minute.

Dan found an old brown paper shopping bag, he wrapped his necessary supplies in with some clothing and carefully packed the shopping bag.

Feeling somewhat better he chose to go back the next morning early, but then remembered he still had another day to kill. Excitement and anxiety did not allow for a restful night. Dan was determined to see this through and lack of sleep was not going to deter him.

The next day almost drove him crazy. He dared not leave the apartment again, yet at the same time he ran out of things to do in the apartment. He mentally reviewed every detail of his plan a dozen times and even that was beginning to annoy him. The television as a distraction was useless. He was sick of the phony entertainment of the talk shows. Even the weather channel was a "Broadway" production in his opinion. A few cat naps now and then finally helped pass the time. With a light supper he forced himself to bed setting his alarm just in case the lack of sleep caught up with him.

Up before the sun he prepared himself for his big day. "Okay, this is it." he said in the mirror.

This morning he chose a different park away from his usual lunch bench for obvious reasons, Ian being foremost. This was a small neighborhood park but with enough trees to be out of sight.

Feeling secure, Dan cleared his mind of all but the familiar country lane just outside of town. Without realizing it he was there, shopping bag and all.

~ ~

Chapter 13

He walked a bit more briskly than he normally did hoping not to meet anyone. He paused momentarily at the café' giving a wink and nod to Eleanor as he passed. Sure she was unnoticed she returned his nod with a flash of five fingers twice. He received the message. She would meet him at ten tonight. Dan continued on to the Worry Free Inn.

Just before he entered his cabin, Travis happened by.

"He must be on the lookout for me all day long." he thought.

"Back again I see." he commented. Slightly startled for not having seen him approach, Dan recovered quickly and went right into his lying mode. He was becoming quite adept at fabricating the truth..

"Yep, needed another break from the hustle and bustle of city life.

I'm making headway though, you know, getting my affairs in order and stuff like that. I think maybe one or two more trips will take care of everything, then I can be here permanently."

Dan detected a small satisfactory glint in Travis's eyes.

"*He seems to be buying my lies.* "He thought.

"That's a good thing. Well I'll let you get on with your day. Have a relaxing one." Travis said over his shoulder as he strolled away.

Dan, feeling good about the believability of his words, entered the cabin putting the shopping bag temporarily under the bed. He grabbed a snack, the fishing pole and made his way to the stream. There was time to kill before Eleanor's visit. With any luck maybe he could fall asleep by the water if the fish don't keep him awake.

As luck would have it Dan did doze off, awakened at dusk by some playful squirrels who thought his shoe laces were fine game.

He slowly rambled back to the cabin and fixed a quick supper anxiously awaiting Eleanors arrival. Dan did some reading of his notes again until finally his watch showed nine forty five. Killing all the lights he waited outside, but not for long. She was a few minutes early and once she spotted Dan she ran to him, throwing herself into his arms almost knocking him down while kissing him with real passion.

"I did so miss you." she whispered.

"And I you." he kissed back.

"Did you really or are you just being nice." she teased.

Dan took her hand and started walking to the stream. Eleanor looked up at him, disappointed.

"I thought we would go inside."

"No, we have to talk, and I don't want to risk my cabin being bugged as you pointed out the last time.

"You're no fun." she pouted.

Dan squeezed he hand in answer.

"Okay." Eleanor smiled in reply. "I carried out my assignment, Boss. I passed the word on our verbal communication tree and received answers. There will be twenty two of us, not counting yourself."

"That's better than I expected. Are you sure that's everyone?"

"To the best of my knowledge. At least for this area. I cannot vouch for other area's or countries."

"Unfortunately we can not concern ourselves with them at this point."

Eleanor looked at Dan again saying;

"I know you're right, I just hate the thought of leaving them behind."

"As do I." Dan replied. "But this whole affair is much to big for just a few people to fight."

She smiled acceptance and remained silent.

"Now for some details of the plan I devised. I have written a description of a place for us to return to without making it too obvious. Pass this along to your tree, have them learn it well then destroy the paper. We also need to know the where about's of Ian and Ted. They must be here in this world when we depart."

"You really did do some planning." Eleanor complemented.

"I also have a bag of necessary supplies in my cabin. I'm hoping you can take it with you tonight. I don't trust it in my cabin. I think it will be safer with you. That is if you don't mind."

"Well, I don't know now, that may require an extra kiss." she bargained.

"I think perhaps we could possibly arrange for something like that."

"Possibly ?" she questioned.

Before she could protest any further Dan had her in his arms kissing her. The kiss ended with Eleanor out of breath.

"Anything else I can demand payment for ?" she smiled.

Back to being serious Dan spoke quietly;

"Try and get this word out as soon as possible, and the location of Ian and Ted. Let's go back to the cabin now."

"I like that idea." Eleanor whispered as she moved closer to him."

"I have to give you the supply bag." he added.

"I said you were no fun." she pouted again.

Dan put his arm around her shoulders and pulled her closer to him as they strolled to the cabin.

"We'll have our time but right now we must maintain clear heads and alertness.

Knowing he was right again she put her arm around his waist and gently squeezed,

"Thank you." she purred.

Making sure no one was around, the transfer of the supplies was made and with one last gentle kiss Eleanor was on her way home.

"I'll see you for breakfast." he called after her.

Half turning to him she smiled and winked. Dan watched her fade away in the darkness.

~ ~ ~ ~

Dan did not have a restful night because of confused thoughts. First and foremost the escape from this other world and whether or not his plan would work. Then, of course there was Eleanor forever popping into his head.

Up early Dan was reviewing for the umpteenth time, the plan he devised.

"I hope this works." he mumbled out loud. "It has to work." he added. "What do we do if it doesn't work ? What happens if we get caught ? I wonder what the "They" will do with us ?

He shook his head to dislodge these thoughts. I must remain positive he told himself.

Dan showered and shaved, looking forward to breakfast with Eleanor. Not exactly with her but at least he can see her. He left the cabin hoping not to see Travis. He felt lucky with his walk to the café' being peaceful and seeing no one of any consequence. At least he thought not. During his walk his mind drifted to the reentry point he chose. A small out of the way park on the Palisades of New Jersey, across the Hudson River from New York City, just north of the George Washington Bridge. Dan had figured on accomplishing the transfer relatively early in the morning. Some where between five and five thirty. Not many people would be stirring about at that hour even in the New York - New Jersey area.

He had no idea where these other people came from but that could be easily settled back in the safety of our original home planet.

Down deep inside the nagging thought remained. What was the reason for the recruiting invasion. If that's what it was ? Why the secrecy ? Most importantly, who or what are they ?"

Dan put aside these disturbing thoughts as he arrived at the Café'. He got his wish of not many patrons as of yet. This would give him time to chat with Eleanor albeit limited. She was all smiles as he entered followed by a loving wink undetectable to the other occupants. Dan went to a corner table which appeared to give him some privacy. Eleanor served a gentleman at the counter then made her way to Dan, a full coffee mug in hand.

"Here you are Sir, black with a touch of sugar."

Dan smiled and was impressed that she remembered how he preferred his coffee.

"And for breakfast Sir ?" She smiled knowing she was over playing the little game. He ordered quietly. "Coming right up Sir." she winked and walked to the kitchen.

Alone and quiet, Dan started thinking again. He was having second thoughts about the reentry place he picked out. It might be vacant at that hour of the day but he also had not been there in a few years.

"I really don't know what it looks like presently. Twenty some odd people is and isn't a lot." he thought. Another concern he had was that it was too far away from his apartment. This presented difficulties for travel to get to a safe haven unnoticed. His mind went blank as he looked toward the front window. Eleanor reappeared with his breakfast yet wearing her warm smile.

Dan gazed up at her in a serious mood.

"When do you think you will be free to talk ? I've changed my plan somewhat."

"I can make time later this afternoon." she answered quietly.

"Did you pass out those instructions yet ?

"No, why ?"

"Don't. I'm going to change them. I can meet you about three this afternoon. Let's say by the pond again. No wait, that's too obvious. Do you know the country road leading out of town ? About a half mile there is a meadow with a quiet babbling brook. I'll be there." Now in a louder voice Dan followed with, "Could I get a refill on my coffee please?"

"Right away Sir." she smiled and winked.

~ ~ ~ ~

"Back to the room now for some privacy," Dan said to himself as he left the Cafe' He remembered there was some note paper in the desk table. He would have to write out a thorough description of the new reentry place, and do it twenty three times between now and three PM this afternoon.

On the walk back to the motel he made the decision to use his apartment. He was successful on transferring out, so why not on returning.

He felt the apartment was large enough, at least the living room was, that is if he moved some furniture. It would be a bit of a squeeze but if everyone cooperated it should be okay.

Finishing his descriptive notes by two thirty Dan would have enough time to keep his appointment with Eleanor.

Luck was with him on his walk to the meeting place, he saw no one to delay him. On the last hundred yards or so he caught up with Eleanor. She turned and ran to his arms with a big welcoming kiss.

"I missed you so, I'm beginning to not like it when you're not around." she offered with a smile that lit up her whole face.

They reached a secluded spot by the creek with Eleanor's arm still around Dan.

"I realized we do not have much time so I'll get right down to business." Dan said.

"I still think you're no fun." Eleanor pouted through a half smile.

Dan laughed then turned serious right away. He handed her the new location descriptions and urged her to get them passed out ASAP. Eleanor could see he was being very serious and put aside her joking manner

"They must all study the location to make it second nature to them." instructed Dan. "I will be going back again this evening to finish up some last minute details."

"How long will you be gone ?" she questioned sadly. "I don't like it when you're gone ." she added.

"For a couple of days. Let's see today is the eighteenth, so I will return early on the twenty first, and I will return to this very spot. The rest is very important, so listen closely. All those wishing to return home must be here between five thirty and six AM. Having well memorized the reentry description. It is my apartment and I honestly think this is possible."

When Eleanor heard "his apartment" her eyes glistened slightly and she smiled.

"This next part is super important. Every effort must be made to make sure both Ian and Ted are here on this world. I will do whatever I can on my part to make that happen. Once we start this there will be no turning back. Please trust me on this. I promise I will get you away from this. You had better go now, and don't forget my goody bag when we meet again. Without that we won't be going anywhere."

Eleanor looked up at Dan, moisture showing in her eyes. She kissed him whispering;

"Please come back to me." With that she turned and walked away in the direction of town.

Dan waited about a half hour and returned the same way.

~ ~ ~

"Travis ! I'm glad I caught you. I hate to leave again, although this should be the last time." Dan said smiling. "I'm going to finish up my affairs and will be back early on the twenty first. I wonder if you could do me a favor and get a message to Ian and Ted Donaldson. I would like to meet them to discuss living arrangements etc. I should be here about six or six thirty. I know that's early, but it will be a total fresh start for me and I want to get settled as quickly as I can."

By now you could see Travis was genuinely happy at hearing Dan's lies.

"I will pass on your message and I am sure Ian will be pleased and will accommodate your wishes."

Dan entered his cabin. "See you soon." he called over his shoulder. *"I really am getting good at this lying stuff. I almost believe my self."* Dan thought.

Safely inside the room he locked the door and transported to his apartment.

Seated with a beer Dan felt tense about all that had just transpired but at the same time felt good about his accomplishments.

"I think another trip to the library is in order to make sure I'm not whistling in the wind about my plan. I know its far from perfect but as a layman it's all I can come up with now. It had to work." Dan told himself.

Dan reached for a few cookies to snack on and fell into bed exhausted.

~ ~ ~

The super polite woman at the library was sort of used to Dan now and indicated the back table was free as soon as she saw him. He thanked her and set about his research. Nothing new came to the surface from his studies nor was there anything that said it couldn't be done. Satisfied for now he left the library for home stopping for Chinese food on the way.

Dan viewed the living room while he ate convincing himself twenty some odd people would fit. He would wait till morning to move furniture.

Dan now had two full days to prepare for the mass transference. One of the first things he realized was that he would require some extra food. Nothing elaborate, just some basics to tide people over till they found there way to permanent places or their original home. Dan also checked his savings account statement. Some extra money wouldn't hurt either. He was sure not too many of them would carry large amounts with them. He would withdraw a few hundred to help out those who needed it.

The bank and shopping ate up a good part of the day. Dan kept to the less traveled streets for the shopping and totally avoided the park, especially his favorite park. He did not need Ian right now.

Back in his apartment in late afternoon, Dan let himself relax for a while. He awoke to a darkened room.

"I guess I was tired." he mumbled almost incoherently.

He reached for the lamp by the chair and blinked at the sudden brightness. His watch showed four twenty AM.

"I should really go to bed now but it's almost time to get up. Dan went in and stretched out on the bed any way, The next thing he knew it was seven forty five.

"I guess I really was tired." he said talking to himself.

There was not much for Dan to do today so he fixed a leisurely breakfast and piece by piece moved some furniture. By eleven the living room was all but empty.

"That about does it." he said aloud as he surveyed his labors. Dan sipped his third cup of coffee and was considering a walk for some fresh air and relaxation but thought better of it. He did not need any outside complications with only a matter of hours to the big moment.

He mentally reviewed his plan again and resigned himself to watching TV. An old western movie caught his fancy and he was finally able to relax for a while. He made due with a sandwich and a glass of milk for supper and after setting his watch alarm he lay down on the bed, clothes and all.

Awake and alert at five fifteen Dan focused his mind on the country road and the hidden pond. He knew he transferred successfully when he felt Eleanor's sweet lips on his.

"I knew you would be early." she bubbled. "And see I remembered your goody bag."

"I knew I could count on you." he smiled

"And you always will be able to." she added.

Still snuggled together they heard a woman's voice behind them.

"Hi Eleanor." was the cheery greeting. "And you must be Dan."

Eleanor and Dan turned in the direction of the voice only to see it was a woman and a man, the first of many arrivals. Dan's first question of course was how well they memorized the transfer sight. Before anything could be said others were arriving in singles and pairs. The word passed that the final instructions would be given just prior to transferring.

The look most prevalent was that of hope mixed with a touch of fear. Fear of being caught. Then what ?

Dan was preparing to address that when a shock of fear touched him also. Daria was there beside him. Eleanor also froze in a worried expression. Anticipating Dan's questions, Daria spoke first.

"There is no need to get upset. I'm on your side." she tried smiling when she said this. "I know what you must be thinking, but please hear me out first. I am here on my own. No one knows I'm here."

Dan sort of drifted away from the group on purpose for more privacy, not to alarm the others.

"How did you find out about this ?" was Dan's first concern.

"I've been in on this from the beginning. The beginning of this wanting to get away from here communications tree."

Alarm showed an Dan's face.

"Please listen to what I have to say and trust me. I know that's asking a lot under the circumstances, but I really am on your side. You might want Eleanor to hear this also."

Hesitating, Dan pondered this for a moment. He then signaled for Eleanor to join them. Once there Dan indicated for Daria to make it quick, they were using valuable time. Daria said she understood this and could assist them.

"To start off I must admit I mislead you in the beginning."

Dan looked directly into Daria's eyes with a cold "Okay let's have it." unfeeling expression. Daria understood his meaning.

"When we first met you asked about my being here, and I said I traveled back and forth between our two worlds just like everyone else. Well, that's not true. I have never transferred from here. I was not allowed. This alternate world to you, is my home world."

This came as a complete surprise to Eleanor and Dan, both were speechless for the moment. Dan recovered the fastest saying;

"And now you're here to squash our escape. You should be real proud of yourself. Does this make you extra points with the powers that be ?"

Dan's anger was obvious and now everyone knew it. He could feel himself wanting to get physical and Daria knew this, showing fright in her eyes

Others arrived making their count complete.

Daria, frustrated herself because of Dan's refusal to listen, raised her voice looking directly at him accusingly.

"You're wrong." she said sharply. "I'm on your side. Please, at least listen to me, we're wasting valuable time."

Eleanor touched Dan cautiously, but lovingly.

"At least listen to what she has to say Dan. We are still in control here, not her."

Dan, a touch embarrassed but hid it well, realized Eleanor was right. He covered her hand with his, and in a more normal tone indicated that Daria proceed. Daria, also relaxed her aggressive stance nodded a silent thank you to Eleanor, and continued.

"I know that you set it up for Ian and Ted to be at the Worry Free Inn early today and I can assure you they are both there and even pleased about it."

This registered with Dan right away.

"Go on." he said softly, and could feel Eleanor relax her grip on his arm.

"I don't know what or who is behind this plot to keep you here. I do know though I don't like it. I'm frightened by it. This is all new to me. For a long time now I have been listening to everyone's stories about your world, and it sounds wonderful."

Yet again, Dan was surprise by her comment.

"Yes, it sounds hectic at times." she continued, "But it's your own choice. You make your own decisions, something we can not do here."

Daria paused here, letting her words register.

"I'm here to help you." she said looking at her watch. "It's getting late. Ian will not stay there all day waiting for you. He's bound to suspect something sooner or later."

"You're right about that." Dan replied not a hundred percent sure he trusted her yet. "How can you help us ?" he asked. Daria answered his question with a question.

"Are you familiar with Quantum Physics ?"

"I have studied enough, I believe, to hopefully get us all away from here."

Being quite serious now, Daria resumed her questioning, more like statements:

"Then you know parallel universes do exist, and yes one can travel between the two. Of course you know this, you are already experiencing it. Have you studied anything about Coherence ? If you have you know the fabric between parallel worlds can be broken."

Dan was impressed with her knowledge and more so with her now apparent willingness to share.

"Do you have the equipment to do this ?"

Dan hesitantly answered.

"I have something that I think will do the job."

"And if it doesn't ? What then ? she asked authoritatively. You will probably end up like Josh."

This really caught Dan's attention.

"You know what happened to Josh ?" he asked.

"Not exactly. I have not been privy to such information but I don't think he will ever be seen again. Is that what you want for yourself, Eleanor and all these other people here ?"

"Of course not." Dan answered shyly.

"If it does work, you're a better person than most who have tried before."

Dan, for the first time since this all started, suddenly felt uncertain. This feeling showed on his face. Daria picked up on this.

"I thought so." she commented in a non show off way.

"I have with me a piece of electronic equipment that I guarantee will do the job. I have it in the trunk of my car. It is rather heavy so if I could get some help we can set it up and get you people out of here."

Dan thought of this for a moment with Eleanor urging him to go along with her. Still not positive he could trust her, he did however ask a few of the men to give her a hand. Returning from the car Daria asked where the transfer was to take place. She needed the exact spot. Dan gauging the crowd size indicated a clear spot near the pond.

Daria proceeded to open and set up the weird looking equipment. There were two small computer screens each showing different electronic patterns.

"Now get the group ready." she ordered. "Once I know that you are ready I will set up a time delay of eight seconds. Your departure place will then close, thus bringing about a total disconnect of the two worlds."

Without waiting for a return comment she asked Dan what kind of a device he planned on using. Sheepishly he showed her the fireworks and timing fuses.

"There is a fifty- fifty chance that this will work but we can put it to better use now."

Dan, with a quizzical look asked how.

"Quickly set up your stuff under my equipment. Set your fuses for fifteen seconds. It's not much but there is enough explosive to render my machine useless. You will still be safely home by the time the explosion takes place.."

"What about you ? Eleanor inquired.

"I'll be alright. I'll come up with some sort of excuse of how you overpowered me before I could sound the alarm."

"Will they believe that." asked Dan knowing the answer would be no.

"Don't worry, I'll manage somehow."

"Is it because you have someone here that you can't leave ?" asked Eleanor.

"No, I have no one to care for, or to care for me." answered Daria with tear filled eyes. Now get your group together and I'll start the countdown,"

Dan gathered all with arms linked so that all were one unit. He looked at Eleanor who understood his wishes and nodded her approval.

He turned to Daria and said okay, then watched her start her apparatus. Once positive of it functioning he grabbed Daria by the arm and pulled her to the group at which time Eleanor hooked her arm. Dan yelled "NOW" and the concentration began. Daria did not have time to struggle free.

~ ~ ~ ~

Dan's living room was suddenly filled with warm, very happy people. The time was six forty five.

Every one was patting each other on the back, shaking hands and hugging. Daria seemed frightened but Eleanor happily drew her into her arms to comfort her.

"You're safe now, No harm will come to you. We will see to that."

~ ~

"I know it's a bit crowded folks, but at least we're all home.

Try and make yourself comfortable while we figure out travel plans to where you want to go."

As it turned out more than half the group were from the Metropolitan area and were already making plans to leave. Dan supplied the necessary money and made sure that they all had his contact information. They agreed a reunion at a later date as yet undecided and would be a good idea.

By four that afternoon there were only nine people left including Dan. Six would be leaving the next day by bus, train and plane to their homes in other states. That would leave only he, Eleanor and Daria. Dan was looking forward to some intimate alone time with Eleanor, but he could not just throw Daria out. After all he did bring her here sort of against her will.

"Well folks what say we try and settle for the rest of the day and tonight. I guess food would be the next order of business." Dan put forth.

Eleanor jumped in excitedly with;

"That's right up my alley. Your kitchen is smaller than I'm used to but I'm sure we can make due.."

"Please allow me to help." volunteered Daria as did the other two women.

"I'm not stocked up with very much right now but I can go to the store. You tell me what you want and that's what we will do." Dan smiled at Eleanor.

After searching the cabinets and refrigerator Eleanor made a list and handed it to Dan.

"Be back in a jiffy." he said heading for the door.

Two of the other men joined him, both agreeing they wanted to get the feel of the real New York City. The remaining people set about setting up places for everyone to eat. Daria appeared suddenly shy. She was not used to being able to do what ever you wanted without being watched or told how to. Eleanor picked up on this and put her arm around her shoulder.

"Every thing's going to be just fine now. You'll see. You're safe now so try and relax."

She said this softly with a smile. The other two women joined in the cheering up party which freed up Eleanor to get dinner started.

In less than an hour Dan and company returned, arms full of goodies including several bottles of wine. With the kitchen buzzing with activity Dan switched on the TV in time to catch the evening news.

"OFFICIAL'S ARE NOW REPORTING THAT MINOR COSMIC DISTURBANCES REPORTED EARLIER THIS MORNING WAS ATTRIBUTED TO SOLAR FLARE ACTIVITY. IT WAS SHORT LIVED WITH NO REAL DISRUPTION OF POWER. NO DAMAGE WAS REPORTED. NOW FOR THE SPORTS, HERE'S MIKE- - - - ."

Dan shut off the TV. Daria calmly remarked;

"I could have told them that."

Questioning looks showed on every ones face. Daria realized this so as an explanation she stated;

"I'm a Quantum Physicist. With an advanced degree in Cosmology."

She said this proudly with a smile. Dan quietly whispered to her,

"That explains a lot. Thank you."

Daria smiled back almost embarrassed.

It wasn't long before Eleanor announced dinner was ready. It isn't much but it is food thanks to Dan. One of the other gentlemen stood, raised his wine glass offering a toast.

"**H**ere's to our knight and hero in shining armor. We all owe you a lot Dan. Thank you."

Daria stood, now speaking shyly this time;

"**A** very special thanks from me for giving me the chance to really have a life not ruled by others."

Dan felt a slight flush take over his face. He was not accustomed to being singled out for complements.

Conversation was light after dinner with everyone feeling the results of their anxious day. Sleeping arrangements were completed with Eleanor and Daria sharing Dan's bed. Cots, sleeping bags and the couch supplied the rest. It wasn't long before the apartment was enveloped in total quiet.

A full hearty breakfast was put forth by Eleanor with Daria's help. Dan had already arranged for transportation for those leaving and by ten thirty all were on their way. This just left Dan and his two lady friends. Dan poured a second cup of coffee and sat down with a sigh.

"**W**ell, Mr. Wonderful, you did it. You accomplished what you said you would." praised Eleanor.

"No, we did it." Dan suggested as he grabbed each woman's hands and lovingly squeezed. "We might not be here if it wasn't for Daria and her equipment." he added.

"Or Eleanor and her keeping tabs on the message tree." Daria said.

"That was mostly Josh. He started the tree." Eleanor countered.

Dan changing the subject and trying to be serious, said;

"And now what do we do with you young lady."

"I'll get out of your hair as soon as possible." answered Daria.

"And where will you go ?" asked Eleanor. "You know nothing of our crazy world. You're going to have to stay here to take time to get accepted to our ways. Please let us help you get settled. I think the three of us can become great friends."

Daria feeling a bit embarrassed looked at Dan doubtfully.

"What she said." he answered with a smile.

Daria appeared to relax with that and joined in the smiles. With everyone relaxed Dan spoke again.

"Now that there is only three of us, there is plenty of room here in the apartment. I think we can all be comfortable here until we get our lives back in order."

The two women agreed with Dan and thanked him for his generosity, though Dan thought he detected a hint of disappointment in Eleanor's eyes. He was a bit disappointed himself not to be able to be alone with Eleanor, but the priority of the situation took precedence. They then proceeded to discuss plans for getting Daria settled. Because of her credentials, Dan figured on not having too hard a time in finding her employment. There are not too many Quantum Physicists roaming around.

~ ~ ~ ~ ~ ~

The rest of the week was pleasant and relaxing. They took in some sights of the city and Dan even gave a quick tour of his studio and art work.

One evening after dinner during light conversation with Daria, Dan mentioned trying to go back to the other world just to see if whether or not the connection was truly broken. Daria appeared slightly alarmed but recovered her poise instantly and speaking in a soft professional voice said;

"I don't think that would be a very good idea. I have heard stories about that happening before and these people have been lost forever. Promise me you will not try that. You are much too important to both Eleanor and I. We would not want anything to happen to you."

Dan smiled and accepted her words. This relaxed Daria even more. Eleanor joined them from the kitchen.

"What are you two looking so happy about." she asked.

"Nothing." Daria answered. "Just totally relaxed after such a great meal."

Eleanor beamed a broad smile as she sat next to Dan holding his hand.

Dan noticed a quick eye exchange between the two women. At first his mind dismissed it as a touch of jealousy.

That night alone in the living room Dan's thoughts drifted back to Daria's comments. Her explanation sounded logical yet there was still a seed of doubt in his mind. Not exactly about her explanation but the alarmed air she took on. Deep inside he felt something was just not right, but exactly what he had no idea. He finally drifted off to sleep but awoke the next morning to the same nagging doubt.

A friendly breakfast was enjoyed by all. Dan then went into a preplanned act.

"**O**h my! Look at the time. I have a photo shoot engagement this morning at ten thirty. I almost forgot about it until I checked my appointment book this morning. It will probably take me about four and a half hours to complete. I should be back by three thirty the latest. You two lovely ladies make yourselves at home and enjoy the day. See you tonight and perhaps we can go out to dinner. There are so many great restaurants in this city we may have difficulty choosing." He smiled.

Eleanor moved to his side hooking her arm in his and gently kissing him.

"**T**here will be more waiting for you when you get back." She whispered.

Daria appeared embarrassed and a bit jealous. Dan kissed her cheek as he went to the door.

"**B**ehave, you two." he quipped.

*"**N**ow I'm really getting confused."* Dan thought to himself once outside. *"Why do I have doubts about Daria's sincerity. After all she did help us all escape. There is also a strange connection between the two women. It almost looked like a touch of jealousy but I really think there is more to it than that. Something feels very strange."*

"I'm glad I'm alone now." he said out loud. "I need time to put my mind back in order."

Force of habit he made his way, without thinking, to his favorite park bench, stopping first for a bag of chips to feed the pigeons. They always helped him think. It had been a while since he had been here but every thing was as it always was. It might have been his imagination but it appeared as if the pigeons missed him and were happy to see him back.

Dan smiled as the birds flocked to his feet vying for the chips he scattered. He knew it was not good for their diet but he felt good again about feeding them.

Even though he was a bit troubled with his thoughts of Daria Dan sat back and relaxed, truly relaxed. His life was hectic for a while going between both worlds but now that was over and done with. This world was not so bad after all.

The gentle cooing of the pigeons helped Dan's eyes close as he took a deep soft breath. Not meaning to but his thoughts went to the quiet country lane of the other world.

"I knew curiosity would bring you back."

Startled, Dan opened his eyes to find himself facing Ian on the same country road.

"You had to find out for yourself, didn't you ?" inquired Ian.

Recovering from the surprise he asked Ian directly.

"Now what are you going to do with me ? Do I disappear like Josh and others ?" Dan asked matter of factly.

"Slow down Pal, you've got it all wrong. I'm the good guy."

Somewhat taken aback by this statement Dan's mind was going every which way trying to determine what was real.

"Did everybody arrive safely ? I expect they did." said Ian

"Then why ask." replied Dan annoyed at the comments.

"I know this must be very trying at this moment. You don't know if you can trust me or not. You don't know if you believe me or not."

The two men stared at each other silently. Dan broke that silence.

"Go on."

"Tell you what." Ian said. "Let me suggest we both go back to your world, or perhaps I should say our world. Our real world. Maybe you will be more comfortable there."

"Perhaps." replied Dan cautiously.

Before Dan could say anything further Ian faded away. *"I hope I'm not trapped here now."* he thought. Rather than dwell on that he pictured his park bench and the pigeons. Sensing a presence next to him Dan turned to see Ian sharing his special bench.

"Feel safer now ?" Ian asked in an unthreatening tone.

Dan actually did feel safer but chose not to say so.

"Forgive me for playing games." Ian continued. "You're right, you deserve some answers and a full explanation. Well, at least as full as I'm allowed to go."

"I wonder what he means by that." ran through Dan's mind.

In a more reasonable frame of mind Dan looked directly at Ian, observing what body language he could, saying:

"I'm listening."

Ian paused momentarily, obviously putting together his thoughts.

"Believe it or not I work for the Federal Government. Yours and my Federal Government. It is a unique and special group of individuals gathered together to investigate connections with extraterrestrials. This group was originally formed in nineteen forty seven because of the Roswell incident.

The group lay dormant from the mid sixties till the early two thousands. ET incidents seemed to surface again, as evidenced by these parallel worlds."

Dan listened spellbound by the story, not knowing whether to believe it or not.

"I know you yourself have studied some Quantum Theory, enough to realize that this is a possibility. Well I'm telling you now it is more than a possibility. It is a reality. You, yourself have witnessed it. You have been a physical part of it."

"That was because of you. You dragged me into it." Dan answered quickly. He had no idea what made him say that and in such an accusatory tone.

"That may have been the case. But you did not fight the idea." answered Ian in a soft non-belligerent voice.

Dan was suddenly sorry he spoke the way he did, but did not apologize. However he did take over the conversation.

"Look, let's put all the cards on the table. Who are you ? Really. I know who you said you were but where is the proof of that?"

"I can easily supply that if you have the time."

"Why do I need time ?"

"Because, my doubting friend, it is many blocks from here. If you walk with me I will take you there."

Dan glanced at his watch and decided he did not have the time right now.

"What about tomorrow , or are you going to disappear to your other world ?"

"I didn't want to put this off too long but if it's going to take tomorrow to convince you, then so be it."

Ian took a piece of paper from his wallet and wrote an address on it.

"Go to this address and ask for me. Ian Hathaway. How does ten in the morning sound ?"

Dan took the paper and agreed on ten A.M. Without another word Ian turned and walked away. Dan followed with his eyes until he was totally out of sight. He sat back on the bench and casually watched the pigeons.

"What have I got myself mixed up in now ?" he thought. *"Perhaps by morning I will have a clear head."*

Remembering the two women at his apartment he turned to home. "Not a word to either one about Ian." he warned himself..

He was welcomed home by both as if he had been gone for days instead of just a few hours. Dan felt rather overwhelmed by all this loving attention. He even thought he could become accustomed to it but also knew it couldn't last. To avoid too much cloistered alone time with them he suggested they go out to a nice restaurant for dinner. Luckily for him they both agreed wholeheartedly. In no time at all they were ready.

His place of choice was an upscale steak house with a superb wine menu. Dan was pleased with his choice because they lingered there for many hours with the two women well wined. He himself was feeling a wee bit mellow but paced his wine sips accordingly. He wanted to try to keep a clear head so he didn't trip himself up. At least until he heard more from Ian.

Dan, as innocently as possible kept the wine flowing for the ladies. Eventually after running up a sizeable restaurant tab for only three people they decided they should head for home. Dan settled the bill for just over two hundred and fifty dollars. He hoped it was worth it to keep the ladies off guard for now. By the time they returned to the apartment it was obvious he plan worked rather well. Both women were tipsy and already slurring their words. Without much argument he was able to direct them to bed, clothes and all.

Now with some free time and a head not too foggy he mentally reviewed his run in with Ian. This was quite a turn around of circumstances. He was confused as to who the bad guy really was. Making himself comfortable on the sofa, Dan also drifted off to sleep.

Chapter 14

Dan had just finished making coffee when both Daria and Eleanor entered the kitchen.

"**A**nd he cooks for himself. How lucky can a girl get ?" Eleanor stated accompanied by a huge smile. She walked directly to Dan and kissed him on the cheek at the same time squeezed his hand. Daria followed suit with a kiss on the other cheek.

"**Y**ou ladies are awfully loving this morning." he commented.

"**Y**ou make that very easy." replied Eleanor.

"*Here comes the shmoozy stuff.*" thought Dan. That thought alone confirmed his wanting to meet with Ian again. Keeping the conversation light Dan offered.

"**I** was just going to fix breakfast before I go out. Can I serve you two ladies also ?"

"You're leaving us again ?" pouted Eleanor.

"Sorry, but I do have a business commitment to attend to. I promise you my undivided attention this afternoon."

"I'll forgive you this time but I'm going to hold you to that promise. Let me fix breakfast first." Eleanor replied.

"Is there anything I can do to help." joined Daria.

Dan cleaned up and dressed while both girls prepared breakfast. While eating Dan avoided a few questions of things he did not want to get into at this point. He rushed through his tasty meal and took his leave with both women still at the table.

Outside he breathed a little easier and aimed his way to the address Ian had given him still puzzled about all the secrecy. The brisk twenty minute walk brought him to his destination where he received a bit of a shock when he read the office sign. "Federal Bureau of Investigation" Now even more confused he entered, showed ID and passed through the metal detector.

As requested he asked for Ian Hathaway and was escorted to a second floor office that housed two desks and an assortment of file cabinets, large and small.

Ian greeted Dan at the door,

"I wasn't sure you would make it. You seemed unsettled yesterday."

"I think I still am." answered Dan. "But my curiosity is overwhelming."

"To answer your first question, yes, I am employed by the FBI and have been for some time." Ian volunteered.

"I wish I knew how he did that." Dan thought to himself. "So why are you involved with me." Dan asked straight out.

"I like that." replied Ian, "Immediately to the point. Sit down Mr. Morgan, or can I call you Dan ?"

Dan nodded his approval to the question as he made himself comfortable in the chair facing the desk. He scanned the rather sterile room while Ian made his way to his own chair

"Now Dan, let me tell you a story. It will sound like science fiction, but believe me it's not. You yourself experienced a small parallel world or universe, if you will. You were there. You were able to travel back and forth freely."

Dan was about to interrupt but Ian held up his hand to stop him.

"Please let me finish."

Dan shook his head affirmatively and remained silent.

"You have obviously read up on some Quantum theories, otherwise you would not have agreed to this meeting. You know this is real and your research has confirmed that this was possible. Now for your next question you're thinking about. Why you ? Well, I had seen you a few times in the park and kind of picked up on your thoughts, and yes extra sensory perception is real." Ian laughed lightly interjecting, there are many more who think the same way about the rat race, particularly here in the city.

Now Dan did interrupt rather vehemently.

"In other words what you're telling me now was part of the same big spiel you gave me a while back. How you met this guy accidently and how you were drawn into the other world. I guess part of your con job to get me to work for you. How many others were in on this charade. I wonder how you sleep at night. I'm even a bigger fool for believing you.

"Let me continue my story, please."

Dan nodded and sat back.

"We have been aware of this parallel world for quite some time and have been trying to keep tabs on the comings and goings. To this date we are still not sure what their exact mission is, though we do feel that it may not be in the best interest of our planet. The one you and I are a real part of. To cut the story short for times sake, it was decided to plant agents there to learn as much as possible concentrating on the intent and purpose of their mission, friendly or not. As an added bit of information, this was not an easy decision nor did we make it alone. This was mutually planned by our world wide counterparts along with us. Other nations were faced with this similar threat, if indeed that is the right term to use."

Dan was feeling considerably disturbed by what he was hearing. Not only did he lose his paradise getaway, but now a possible alien threat of his whole existence. He worked at controlling his emotions in order to hear more of the unbelievable tale.

Ian allowed Dan to digest his story thus far. He knew this was a lot to swallow. He poured each of them a cup of coffee before he continued.

Dan spoke up sarcastically.

"And I suppose you're one of those agents ?"

"As a matter of fact I am, as was Josh. That is until they discovered his real identity."

"And that's when he went on vacation ?"

"Exactly. That was something we did not anticipate. He was one of our best."

"If you did all this careful planning how could you not anticipate such a move. It would seem to me if you knew there could be a possible threat to our worlds security, closer and more adequate precautions would have been put in place."

"You are absolutely right Dan." Ian answered calmly not feeling the least bit threatened by Dan's verbal accusations. "And you, thinking like that is why you are here today."

Dan stared directly at Ian, confusion showing in his expression.

"And just what is that supposed to mean." Dan questioned defensively.

Ian, retaining his poise, calmly replied.

"There is no need to get upset Dan, just give me a chance to explain. You're thinking, your caring, you're helping others escape who knows what kind of future, confirms my original judgement of you, and that was long before you transferred to the other world. I know you consider the other people were recruiting for who knows what reason, but I or we , to be more precise, were recruiting also. Specifically people like yourself. People we felt we could trust to be real and not found out to be part of our official security network. You were the ideal person, and you yourself proved it with what you just accomplished."

Dan sat there not knowing what to think. Ian let this moment of silence stretch a little bit.

"Now." he continued, "I'll fill you in on the part that will definitely upset you. We used you- - - , We used you because you were the right person for the job."

Dan now had an unexpected, startled look on his face. He didn't know whether to be elated or angry. Ian, after gauging Dan's expression went on.

"Josh further confirmed that we had picked the right person."

Dan had felt a connection with Josh but did this make it alright to use him this way. He was about to say something when Ian held up his hand again.

"There's more. And I know this is really going to shock you, so I apologize beforehand."

Dan stared intently, waiting.

"Every one of those you just helped join our world were not from our world. They were agents of our parallel planet. They came here to infiltrate our world. Reasons for this are still unknown to us.."

Dan's mind was going wild with questions, with concern and with anger. He even thought of Eleanors warm kisses and embraces. After a short pause Ian added.

"Yes, even her. In fact as far as we can figure so far, she is one of the leaders. How important a figure we have not ascertained yet, but important enough to have run that whole settlement where we both operated."

Dan's thoughts went to Daria.

"Daria was nothing more than a stooge who did exactly as she was told. When she failed to seduce you Eleanor jumped in to complete the job. They needed you to complete the transfer from their world to ours."

Dan, still slightly upset and angry, held up his hand.

"Wait a minute. What about your part in all this. You were with them and were a major influence on me. Then there was the time in the restaurant with Daria. After I questioned her about travel she had to check with you for an answer. I saw the two of you talking. What was the big secret for, and why was she going to you for instructions."

Backing off a bit, Dan spoke a little more calmly.

"It seems to me you're involved in this plot up to your neck. Perhaps you are this other world's plant here with this agency."

Ian sat back and smiled.

"That my friend is a logical conclusion and under the same circumstances I also would have come to that conclusion. You can put your mind to rest on that issue. My credentials here with the agency go back a long way, almost twenty years I believe. Josh was with the group even longer. We have yet to figure out how they found him out. He was not one for making slip ups."

As Ian paused Dan spoke up;

"If what you say is true why do they not cross over to our world by themselves. Why did they need me, or anybody for that matter. I"m sure they could have accomplished this on an individual basis and we would have been none the wiser. And again I ask, What is their purpose ? The fact that I have been used by you is bad enough but also being used by an alien people is very upsetting. I don't know what the truth really is any more. Can I believe you or should I believe you after all that has just happened."

Dan could feel himself getting red faced even though he was working at restraining himself.

Ian, raising his arms as if surrendering offered;

"I wish, or rather we wish we had those answers. Those and a lot more to satisfy all our questions."

Ian arose from his chair. "Come walk with me. What I am about to show you is highly classified but I truly believe you need to see this."

Leaving the office they walked down a corridor to a secure room. Ian swiped his ID card for entry along with finger print identification. The door opened electronically and the pair proceeded through. Dan saw they had entered a large windowless room. There were a few small offices to the sides but the bulk of the room was large tables and quite a few banks of computers and other electronic plotting machines. One wall was a rather detailed world map holding identifying flags at key spots throughout the world, New York city being one of them.

"These flags, I'm sure you have surmised, are the critical sights we are dealing with in this other world crisis. Our sister agencies in other countries are in full cooperation and as vigilant as we are."

Dan again asked the obvious question.

"What is their mission ?"

"That we have yet to ascertain."

"What efforts have been made to contact them."

Ian answered cooly.

"We have had plants such as Josh under cover only to find that they disappear."

"Why undercover ? Why not just extend the hand of friendship first and ask what their purpose is ? They could possibly be perfectly harmless. Just an exploratory venture of the galaxy to learn or to teach."

Ian looked at Dan with a very perplexed expression as if Dan was ignorant about the world. Dan picked up on this right away and spoke with out hesitation.

"If you don't mind me saying so, I personally find that attitude typical of all our bureaucracies. Always trying to out guess a situation or person. You don't always have to think the worst of things. Yes, give consideration to the worst but try considering the other side before going off the deep end with danger and threat. There are others in this galaxy and most likely in the universe who know more than the government bureaucracy. Put yourself in their shoes. Picture yourself or your colleagues on a space exploration mission, landing on an unknown, far away planet with nothing but peaceful intentions only to find you are suspected of evil intentions for no reason.

By now many people were staring in disbelief of his tirade, calm though it was. Ian broke into a slow grin which now confused Dan even further.

"Now I know we have the right man."

"The right man for what ?" Dan questioned.

"Why to be our emissary." Ian continued, still smiling. The others in the room were also now smiling.

Now it was Dan's turn to be dumbfounded. Feeling like a fool after giving his behavioral speech, his mind filled with questions.

"I know you have many questions, but before you or we get into that, permit me to continue our tour."

Dan settled once again politely agreed and even added that he would keep his mouth shut. For now anyway.

"Fair enough." replied Ian. "I'll listen to all you have to say when we are finished.

~ ~ ~ ~

The next hour slowly ticked away as the pair moved from table to table, computer to computer with Ian explaining all, apparently holding nothing back. It appeared to Dan that the other participating countries were approaching this self made crisis exactly the same way. There had been no friendly overtures made to the other world visitors. What was even worse Dan discovered a few had been arrested and were being held in secret. Ian was hush- hush on their treatment after that, which did not sit too well with Dan. He knew he would definitely be questioning that later. He surmised from the guarded information he was being given that there were already beings from the other world among the peoples of other countries. Apparently the escapees that transferred with him were the first in the U.S.A. He reminded himself to question that later also.

Finally they ended up back at Ian's office and within minutes were joined by another agent. Dan guessed him to be Ian's supervisor or at least in some position of authority. He introduced himself as Gary Curtis.

"Okay ! Let's begin." he said hurriedly. "Mr. Morgan, or may I call you Dan ?"

Dan nodded his approval even though Gary continued, not paying attention to Dan's physical reply.

" I know that you may have a few questions. I'm sure we can get these answered quickly, I have other appointments."

Dan thought this Gary fellow to be cold, not genuinely interested in what was going on and rather full of himself. He was beginning to tire of the whole matter. Deciding to deal directly with Mr. Curtis, Dan spoke firmly, letting his displeasure be known.

"Good, then I will begin, but not with my questions."

Gary Curtis looked at Dan with annoyance showing on his face.

"First of all Mr. Curtis, I don't like your attitude. I'm not one of your flunkies. I'm here voluntarily to try and understand the situation which you obviously don't."

Ian was now sporting a quiet smile in his facial expression, enjoying Dan's words.

"I want to cooperate with your investigation but not as one of your stooges. I do, believe it or not, have a mind of my own which I use to sort out things, in what I think, is a logical manner. Your people got me involved in this and I've had enough of being one of your puppets. Now, you either fill me in on everything to my satisfaction or I'm gone and you can find yourself another monkey whose strings you can pull.

And to further clarify my point, to reiterate, your people involved me without my knowledge of what or why. I don't like being used. You had no right to do such a thing. So, now if I have made myself clear, I will pursue the answers to my questions."

Dan became quiet not taking his eyes from Gary Curtis who was now red faced and obviously ready to explode. Explode he did not but stormed out of the room. Ian had all he could do to keep from laughing out loud. Once the door was closed behind Gary he did laugh while saying,

"I couldn't have said it better myself. How he ever became a supervisor no one knows. Now, maybe you and I can continue undisturbed."

Dan now began to smile himself.

"Okay, my first and most obvious question. Why there was no attempt to talk directly to the visitors ?"

"I have no answer for that my friend. It was suggested by a few of us but was frowned upon by the upper echelon. Why ? I don't know. Our orders are only to observe."

"Now moving to question number two. Those in other countries that were arrested. Why and what happens to them."

"Fear of the unknown, I guess." Ian answered. "And what happened to them after arrest is still a mystery, The other governments have not shared all their activities with us which we find typical in many joint ventures."

"Third and most important to me. Why did such a large group transfer from the other planet with me ? And why me /

"A fair enough question, Dan, and I guess you really deserve an honest answer."

"I think I do." replied Dan instantly.

"Well, I learned from some of their meetings that because New York was such a large city they would need numerous people to mix with our population. To what end I do not know yet."

"And why me ?"

"It was decided that it would be more believable with someone like you who thought they were helping their own kind escape. All of those who already left your apartment have one of our agents following. We are keeping tabs on all their movements and contacts."

"Have you learned anything yet ?"

"Not really, it's too early to know what they are up to."

"If anything." Dan followed bluntly.

Ian caught on to his meaning.

"So what are your plans, besides just observations and what kind of threat are you expecting and what kind of defense are you preparing ?"

"Now you're asking questions I have no answer for, nor do I think anyone does." Ian stated.

"I for one don't find much satisfaction or confidence in that." remarked Dan cooly. "Putting my personal feelings aside what kind of a plan do you have for me."

"Nothing like getting straight to the point." Ian smiled. "To be honest, since you are involved, semi romantically with Eleanor....."

"I think that's wishful thinking on your part." Dan interrupted.

Ignoring Dan's comment Ian continued. "Since you are already romantically involved we thought you would be able to gain their confidence and learn whatever you could regarding their purpose here."

Dan remained silent as if pondering Ian's proposal. When he thought an adequate period of time had lapsed he looked at his watch and then turned to Ian.

"I have to seriously think about this. I don't think I can give you an answer right now. Let me sleep on it."

Dan quickly stood and excused himself heading for the door. Ian spoke again but Dan pretending not to hear, kept moving. As he passed Gary's office he received a hateful glare. He smiled back and waved goodbye.

Once back on the street, Dan inhaled deeply. He figured a good breath of fresh air would help clean away the uncomfortable, dirty feeling he was left with from his meeting with the Government.

Chapter 15

Dan walked slowly, taking a round about way back to his apartment. His mind was spinning with unanswered questions. He couldn't believe the game playing that was being performed by the government agencies. Not just foreign countries but our own. *"I thought we were supposed to be more civilized than that."* Thinking about this and all that had just transpired he made up his mind. *"The authorities won't do it, so I will. To me it's the only thing that makes sense."* Resigning himself to finding the truth he went more directly to his apartment.

The greeting upon arrival was as warm today as was yesterday. Perhaps even warmer from Eleanor who seemed to want to linger in his arms.

With the loving preliminaries over Dan became serious.

"Ladies, we have to talk. Please sit down and listen to all I have to say before you react. This is not going to be easy for either of us."

The two women looked at each other then back to Dan. They were not looks of alarm but of curiosity. Dan directed both to the sofa while he took the chair opposite.

"I almost don't know how to begin so I am going to be very open and direct. I don't believe either of you have been open or forthright with me. I know who you are, or at least I think I know who you are."

Dan took note of their reaction to his statement and their questioning looks to each other. This is not the home planet to either of you, is it ? You are both from the parallel world to the earth. Am I correct ?"

Here Dan paused, watching the girls reaction and awaiting an answer. Daria appeared upset and nervous. Eleanor remained poised and unshaken, and looking directly into Dan's eyes asked;

"Why do you ask such a question ?"

Taken slightly aback by this answer he followed with,

"Why are you answering my question with a question ? All I want here is the truth. I am not here to judge you, good or bad. I just want the truth. I am not one of the bad guys.

Hosting a slight smile Eleanor answered;

"**Y**ou have been in touch with Ian again haven't you ?"

Not wanting to appear as hiding anything Dan answered directly.

"**Y**es I have but not exactly by choice."

Daria, acting very nervous, stuttered out;

"**Y**ou went back to the other world didn't you ?"

Dan answered immediately.

"**Y**es and as you can see I returned safe and sound. Not to worry, I'm perfectly okay. I met Ian there and he returned here with me."

Eleanor interjected right away.

"**A**nd you spent the morning with him at the FBI office, correct ?"

Dan was suddenly taken aback by her statement.

"**W**hat ever he told you, there is another side to that story. He is the reason we are here."

Here to do what ?" Dan questioned cautiously.

"**T**o get away from him." replied Daria, remaining in her upset state.

Eleanor reached over to hold Daria's hand hoping to calm her. Dan was suddenly filled with questions confusing him even more. Taking a deep breath he said.

"Okay, I'm listening, what is your story ? And why do I get the impression you're going to say Ian and the FBI don't exist."

"A very astute observation, Dan. You're right, you should get the whole story."

"The real story." Daria added sheepishly.

It looks like we're going to be home for the evening ladies. Why don't we fix ourselves some snacks and I'll open a bottle of wine." Dan said in a comfortable tone along with a friendly smile. Eleanor joined in the smile and eventually coaxed one from Daria. Eleanor stood up, moved to Dan and gently kissed him on the cheek.

"You're so easy to love." She turned and headed for the kitchen. Dan moved to Daria and gently touched her hand.

"I will not let anything happen to you. I promise."

As if this was the magic touch her whole body appeared to relax and the strain left her face.

In no time a variety of foods appeared on the table along with three glasses which were being filled by Dan. He, for reasons he did not understand, suddenly felt comfortable and at ease. Either the two women had fabricated another story or he could possibly get real answers.

The trio, resettling and more relaxed as they sipped their wine, looked at each other with smiles deciding who was going to kick off this uncomfortable conversation. Dan made the opening remarks.

"This is what I know so far. I have transported numerous times back and forth between parallel worlds, both physically and mentally. Correct me if I am wrong, but I surmise both of you are from the other world."

Affirmative nods were given.

"I have also done some research and have confirmed that Quantum theories accept and allow for such transferences, though they refer to smaller particles. I have also come to the conclusion that you and your world are most likely further advanced than we are, hence the travel here."

Eleanor repeated her positive nod.

"Now comes the confusing part. Number one, why all the theatrics of staying and leaving ? Number two, What really happened to Josh ? Number three, other countries were mentioned. Is that real or just another fabrication to keep me guessing ? Number four, Just who is Ian and what is his part in all this and what is his relationship with the two of you ? Am I correct in saying it is not a good thing."

Both girls nodded yes, yet again. At least this time it was accompanied with small smiles.

"I'm tired of being subjected to game playing by others. I do not like being someone else's pawn. The final explanation I would like is who exactly are you, where are you from and what is your mission here. So ladies, it's time for the real truth. I must add though, I feel this time we can be totally frank with each other. I do feel a bond between us and I would not want that destroyed in any way."

Big smiles came from both with extra loving eye contact from Eleanor.

~ ~ ~ ~

Eleanor answered without hesitation.

"You are absolutely right Dan. You do deserve an answer, and an honest one. I will do my utmost to live up to and deserving of your trust and patience."

"We both will." Daria answered firmly.

Down deep inside Dan believed them and sat back coddling his glass of wine.

"Let me begin with your last inquiry." stated Eleanor. "We are from a galaxy as far away as you could possibly imagine. We originally resided at the exact opposite end of this ever expanding universe."

"And yes, your assumption is correct, though our species are alike we are far more advanced then your present state." joined Daria. "From what we know of you so far I would guess about two thousand to twenty five hundred years more advanced in both our technology and knowledge of life and the universe."

Eleanor picked up again. "Being of the same species our outward appearance has not changed over time. But internally we have evolved to a point that we have conquered all diseases, mentally and physically that you are still struggling with. I'm sure there may be unknown ailments some where in this universe that we have yet to come across which may be life threatening to us, but I believe we have the ability and resolve to meet it head on and conquer it."

Daria took over the conversation again.

"Our ancestors were once in the dark ages as you are now but through perseverance and pursuit of knowledge we have evolved to a better way of life."

Dan never considered himself to be in the dark ages. After listening to the two women for the last few minutes he figured the old adage, "Everything is Relative" still applied. Daria followed with;

"We have overcome disease, we have no war, we have no crime, yet we are still individuals who may pursue whatever life we want without ridicule. That is until recently."

Dan being quick to catch on offered;

"That being when you came across Ian, correct ?"

"Yes answered Daria with a touch of fear back in her voice.

Eleanor took over then.

"Daria was forced into this terrible charade. There are other loved ones involved. I'll explain later. Back to the mission which started out to be one of enlightenment for anyone we thought could use our guidance for a better world."

"That believe it or not, I can understand." interjected Dan. "And believe me our world could use it. So how did Ian become involved and I'm guessing he was not in your original plan."

"You guessed right again." replied Eleanor.

"Ian is not even one of us." blurted out Daria rather angrily.

Eleanor again made actions to calm her friend while looking at Dan.

"Ian and others are from another world not quite as advanced as we are. There are those from his world who yet pursue power. I imagine because of our totally peaceful nature we were easy to suddenly control. Not all of us, but a few key people of authority. The major population is not even aware that this is taking place. It is just unheard of in our civilization and has been that way for ions." Daria spoke softly;

"Those of us who unwittingly became involved do not even know how to fight back. It's as if it were bred out of our nature."

Dan thought to himself, *"Lucky for you I still know how to fight back."* He quietly observed both women and was convinced they were finally telling the truth. He decided he would bide his time to hear the full story before committing his help.

~ ~ ~ ~

"What about Josh ? How does he fit into all this ?"

Eleanor softly smiled, "Josh was an innocent, like you. He believed in the beginning he was actually going to a less stressful place. But like you he started having doubts and questioned things. When Ian suspected you and he were getting too close Josh just disappeared. We were all told he went on vacation but not all of us believed that story."

"Do you have any idea what happened to him ?" Dan inquired quietly.

"None what so ever." Daria responded.

"Does anyone really know where he came from ?"

"I was probably the closest to him and I got the impression he was from your world here." Eleanor said.

"Did he have a last name or any other way of further identity ?"

"Again the answer is no. Such information was never forthcoming. I'm sorry I can't help you any further with Josh. I just do not know any more about him than you already know. I was really getting to like him too. He appeared to be sincere and genuinely concerned as you."

That hint of a smile showed in her eyes again.

*"I believe she means that. "*thought Dan. He paused for a moment to

let the ladies relax before he asked any more questions. None of three even touched the wine, which he figured was a good thing under the circumstances.

Dan moved to the radio and found some low key soothing music from his CD collection to help ease the tension in the room. As he passed Eleanor returning to his chair she reached out and lovingly squeezed his hand. He gave back the same gentle pressure and smiled before they broke contact.

~ ~ ~ ~ ~

"For the sake of my own curiosity where exactly are you from and how and when did Ian gain control ?"

The women looked at each other as if giving each other permission. Eleanor nodded to Daria, then turned back to Dan, obviously to talk.

"Our original mission, as I mentioned before was one of peaceful intentions. A sharing of our advanced knowledge so to speak. We were not going to get into or use this parallel world or universe theory. Yes we were going to send representatives to live among you. But our intent was to do it openly. Possibly landing a space craft so as not to immediately divulge our superiority. At least not in the beginning. We wanted to share our non violent life.

Eleanor turned to Daria indicating her turn to speak.

"Your galaxy, as all the others, is in constant motion. Your planets and moons orbiting your sun etc. Your galaxy as a whole is also always moving through out the whole ever expanding universe. It takes about two hundred thousand years for your sun and planets to complete an orbit. This change in positions puts galaxies close to others that would not normally be in those positions. This in turn allows travel between galaxies because of that closeness. Remember, the perception of distance looking up at a night sky, for all practical purposes, is undetectable. Our planets distance from yours, considering every day life, is about as far away as too heavenly bodies can be.

Dan sat mesmerized by Daria's explanation. He understood the basic points but also realized her knowledge was way over his head. But she did put it in such a way that he did not feel foolish or inferior. For this he was thankful.

Eleanor picked up their story.

"You asked about Ian and his part in all this. He is from another solar system and different from both of ours. Slightly more advanced than your planet perhaps by a few hundred years but has not yet reached our level of sophistication. He and many others like him are still power hungry and believe that controlling others should be their ultimate goal. It was purely accidental that we made contact with him, or I guess I should say his planet. As I mentioned our intention was peaceful but it turned out to be the chink in our armor as your saying goes. We were not expecting or prepared for such aggressiveness. Especially when it was put upon us by force. We are at the point now that we really don't know what to do. We are not equipped mentally or physically to handle such confrontation."

"But I am." Dan thought.

"There are some from our home that are rethinking our reaching out efforts if it is going to mean reverting to constant conflict."

"That is an understandable reaction and those seeking that path should not be criticized." Dan remarked.

"You seem to understand but not all think as you."

There was a pause and Dan took the opportunity to share some of his thoughts.

"Do you have any idea how many people are involved in the

intrusion on your planet and now on mine ? If I'm going to help you I need to know certain things."

This statement took Daria and Eleanor by surprise. They looked at each other with questioning smiles. Daria spoke excitedly;

"Why would you want to help us after all we put you through ? How can you trust us now ? Why should you trust us now ?"

Both women were quite serious now and appeared concerned and sincere. Eleanor took the lead.

"To the best of my knowledge all those presently involved are here in this area.."

"What about other countries on this globe ?"

Daria answered with a puzzled expression. "Is that what Ian told you ? There are no other places involved on this planet. At least not yet. Their plans were to start here. And once they controlled this country they would then move on to the others. Are you sure you want to get involved with us ?"

Dan chuckled at the question and replied;

"Well you need help and who else is there for you to ask ? Besides this is now involving my planet and I can not let that happen. For all our faults this is still my home.

191

After a short pause Dan continued,

"Are they, by themselves, capable of making the transfer between both worlds ?"

"Why no, why do you ask ?"

"I thought not." Dan replied. "What ever they are trying to accomplish they must do it through you. Is that a correct assumption."

"Yes again." she answered with a questionable grin.

"Do you have a plan in mind ?" Eleanor jumped in excitedly.

"Well sort of." Dan smiled in return. "But I do need a lot of information that is way beyond my understanding. That is where you two come in. I fear time is not on our side. Something must be accomplished before they spread out too much. If we play our cards right perhaps we can put a stop to their conquering ways."

Both women, sporting big smiles answered simultaneously.

"How can we help. Tell us what you need."

All three reached for their respective wine glasses and gave a silent toast.

Chapter 16

For the first time in months, Dan felt a confidence he had not been aware of. He reenforced his promise to both women of his protection yet they must continue their roll as followers of Ian. All three knew Ian was a clever man and that they had to play to his vanity. Dan then focused on Daria because of her knowledge of the working of the universe. His first and most important question was how much longer would the connection to their parallel world be available and more importantly can it be broken permanently.

Without hesitation Daria responded.

"The availability of a parallel connection would be there for a few hundred years. That is if one knows that it even exists."

Dan appeared satisfied with her answer. She went on to part two of

Dan's inquiry.

"The parallel transference between two worlds can be broken, as you yourself learned from your readings. It can be broken but not on a forever permanent basis."

Dan was confused. Even Eleanor appeared puzzled. With a half smile Daria explained.

"Sooner or later as the other worlds evolve, knowledge of the universe such as ours will be attained. But that is something you do not have to worry about in this situation. We are probably talking about many hundreds of years."

Dan smiled his answer.

"I think we can all live with that."

The smile was joined by both ladies.

"I still don't know what you are getting at." said Daria.

"I may not know either, after all I'm very new at trying to save two planets from destruction." joked Dan.

The women laughed along with him.

Looking at Daria again Dan resumed his inquiry; "That was just the basic information I needed. The hard fact is yet to come."

His words intrigued the women.

"For instance how many are here, besides you two ? And can they be identified ?"

Eleanor answered, "Believe it or not the only ones at present are the ones that transported to your apartment, twenty two I believe."

Dan shook his head in agreement.

"And Ian with his advanced team of eight, including Ian. That makes a total of thirty counting Daria and myself."

At this point she could see Dan was lost in thought.

"How did Ian's group get here and when ?"

Daria fielded the question.

"It was about three days before we did. He wanted to set up the fake FBI office before you arrived. It just dawned on me, I don't believe Ian is yet aware of my presence here. Remember you kidnaped me."

Her last words were said with a smile. Dan chuckled at this and asked.

"Are you sorry ?"

"I was at the beginning but I'm not anymore. It feels good to be free again."

"And we're going to try to keep it that way." Dan returned. "Now, and this is important, are Ian and the others able to travel between worlds by themselves ?"

"Ian perhaps but not the others. They need me to facilitate the movement."

"Why Ian and not the others ?"

"Well, like yourself Ian possessed the imaginative brain function to accept and allow such happenings. You, Josh and very few others have this capability."

"To change thoughts for a moment, was Josh transported back to his own world ?"

"No, to the best of my knowledge. I would certainly have known about it."

"Is there any chance he could still be alive ?" Dan pushed.

"I would say a very good chance, we would only have to locate where they are holding him."

"That is good news and we will pursue that later. Now back to the present. Are there any others like you to aid in the transport between worlds ?"

"Yes, quite a few."

Dan's high hopes dropped somewhat on hearing this.

"But none are present in this isolated made up community."

Feeling instantly better Dan's thoughts resumed their wild directions. He paused here obviously concentrating. Both women felt comfortable now and were quiet allowing Dan his freedom of thought.

"This may be a sore subject but I have to know how did Ian get the control he seems to have over you, both of you ?"

Eleanor hesitated a few seconds then spoke as if ashamed such a thing occurred.

I mentioned earlier we are truly a peace loving people. We have conquered all the foibles you are still faced with. We have no standing army, no armies at all. We have a small global navy whose only function is rescue missions. They possess no weapons of any kind. We don't even have police because there is no crime. Compared to your ways we are totally innocent. Technologically and socially advanced, but innocent."

Dan smiled at her honest remarks while answering with;

"**A**nd a wonderful way of life it is. That was the piece I was looking for which led to my first transfer. Little did I know at the time what I was getting involved in."

Eleanor, with genuine sincerity voiced;

"**I** am so sorry we misled you, but----."

Dan stopped her there. "What's done is done. Let's move on to a better future. Back to the present."

Eleanor's eyes held his showing that her love was real.

"**S**o what you are saying is that because of your innocent ways you were easy prey."

"**B**asically that is correct. He and a few others aggresively took control of key people. Hostages you would say in order for us to do their dirty deeds. We never did ascertain the reasons for such control or what their actual goal was."

"**H**ow did you happen upon Ian, or vice- versa ? What planet is he from ?"

"**H**is home planet is just about half way between our two worlds. We were the ones who initiated contact. For the same reason we were coming to your world. To teach, to help, to broaden your knowledge of the living universe. We were here in the late nineteen forties and early fifties by your calendar. What we observed was a people much too backward to accept our advanced knowledge. We kept monitoring your earth since then and you have come a long way in only seventy or so years. We had not planned on Ian being one of our emissary's. That sort of brings us up to date in a quick nutshell."

Dan again paused deep in thought.

"Let me recap for a moment before we go further. Ian is not one of you, nor can he, or any others transport by themselves. They definitely need you as a conduit. Can they go back to their own planet without you ?"

"No, not yet." said Daria. "They are not that advanced."

"Can you transport them all back to their home ?"

"Well-l-l- yes." she answered hesitantly. But that may be difficult to achieve, especially with so many of them now spread out."

"We can work that out I'm sure." Dan volunteered. He stood and paced for a while to the kitchen and back again several times. Eventually returning to his chair he took a small sip of wine and looked at both women.

"I hate to do this to you but you must maintain a connection to Ian.

He still thinks you're here to keep an eye on me. We can not disrupt that belief."

Both Eleanor and Daria appeared slightly upset at Dan's words, particularly Daria..

"No need to get upset. Together we can work this out. I repeat, I will not let anything happen to either of you. That is a promise I will keep no matter what it takes."

Eleanor was now all smiles as usual and you could tell Daria was doing her best to take comfort in Dan's confidence.

~ ~ ~ ~

"This mornings meeting with Ian ended with nothing decided on my part. I said I had to sleep on it. I don't believe Ian was too pleased with me but he also saw fit not to push me. Which sort of tells me he needs me. At least in his mind he needs me and I'm going to play on that need. In order to play his game I need your cooperation which is why you must maintain contact with him. Tell him anything you think he wants to hear. I'm sure the three of us can come up with stories to keep him satisfied. He must be convinced I'm truly under his control or at least his influence."

The women seemed to understand the need for this deception.

"To put it simply." stated Eleanor. "We're going to play his game but turn it back on him."

Dan smiled in answer. "Bingo" he said.

Daria was a bit confused but the thought of getting the best of Ian pleased her.

"Enough of that." Dan commented. "Let's not celebrate before hand, we still have a lot of work to do. Our planning must be foolproof and carried out precisely. So, that being said, let me return to Ian and his group. We need to identify each and every one and their location."

"I may be able to help in that area.. Because I was involved with Josh and the communication tree I do have a list of all that were transported."

"Including the make believe FBI people ?" asked Dan.

"Yes, including them." Eleanor happily replied.

"Then some how you must get in touch with Ian to ascertain their exact whereabouts. I know I'm asking a lot but if we are to succeed we must attend to things we care not to."

The ladies knew this to be true and agreed to play their parts.

"Now once we positively locate all the players we must figure a way to get them all congregated in one place. I know that's not going to be easy and that's just step number one. Step two, which is what I want you Daria, to concentrate on, is to work on a plan or way to transport the whole group, including Ian back to their own world. Let them corrupt each other and leave us alone. And most importantly once they have returned to their own system the connection must be permanently broken. That must be absolute."

Daria instantly thought of the difficulty of such a task but smiled thinking of the final results.

"In the meantime all three of us will continue to play his game."

"I may have to go back to the other world, as quietly as possible of course, to set up such a transfer. I will need access to our tech. labs." mentioned a now enthusiastic Daria.."

"We will work on that and when the time is right we will make it happen." Dan confirmed.

There was a pause with everyone breathing easier. Eleanor spoke softly.

"Then what happens ?"

"**W**ell, I guess the next obvious step is to return you two to your own world to resume your happy lives. I would strongly recommend though that you move on to other worlds with your mission. The planet Earth I do not believe is yet ready for such changes no matter how beneficial they may appear. Possibly wait a few more decades and try again."

Neither of the two women disagreed but Eleanor's expression took on a sudden sadness. As an after thought Dan asked about the present state of transporting.

"**D**oes Ian still have access and if so, can it be stopped, even if it's only temporary ?"

"**I**'m sure we can arrange that but I will need three or four hours to accomplish it." answered Daria.

"**C**an you do that tomorrow ?"

"**Y**es, I believe so."

"**G**ood, then let's do it. I will keep Ian here and busy again to give you the time you need."

Dan paused again thinking. After about five minutes of silence he faced his two companions smiling.

"Enough mental stress for today. Let's drink this fine wine and think about dinner."

No arguments were forthcoming. The ladies moved to Dan each kissing a cheek with a warm "Thank You".

"Come on Daria." urged Eleanor, "Let's see what we can dig up in this room he calls a kitchen."

Dan sat down with his feet up, refilled his glass and leaned back thinking up a story for tomorrow's meet with Ian.

Chapter 17

Dan knew whatever story he came up with would have to be convincing. He had to keep Ian and his "Ner-do-wells" off guard. The girls would have to play their parts well also. Dan was not looking forward to seeing Ian and his phony FBI people but he needed to buy time for Daria to complete her first task on the parallel world. The only off hand plan he could come up with at the moment was one of questions. To keep pounding Ian and his crew with questions as to what his actual job was to be in the whole track down the bad guys scenario. Another added detail he could throw in would be a telephone call from Eleanor while he was with Ian. Just a report in call if you will, to inform Ian that I was being a good boy and had no suspicions as to what he was up to.

The selected music of the CD was finished and as he stood to change it he was informed by Daria that dinner was ready. Eleanor amazed him again by being able to create something so good out of just about nothing.

During dinner Dan outlined his rough plan for tomorrow which was accepted by both. Eleanor advanced some thoughts of her own regarding the phone call. That Dan was out seeing clients drumming up business. Daria joined in with cautions. The possibility did exist that he could be followed. Ian liked to cover all contingencies.

"Why would they want me followed." Dan asked.

"To make sure you weren't going to the real authorities." returned Daria. "After long studies of Ian I deduced that he doesn't trust anyone. Even those that work with him, and probably Eleanor and I most of all."

"That may well be but I'm sure I can convince him otherwise." offered Eleanor smiling. "I will feed him information he can't resist."

"And what would that be." asked Dan.

"The workings of the local government, such as who the key people are. By his own admission he knows nothing of the planet Earth. You still have warring factions and he doesn't know how to handle that. He sees that as a threat to his controlling nature. That's one of the reasons he wanted to stick with your country."

"So I guess in order to bolster your credibility I should also play the same cards, you know feed him information which I know to be true."

"But not for too long a period." warned Daria. "We must seriously work on getting all his agents in one place."

"That brings me to another question." Dan jumped in. "In order for us to transport between worlds we all had to concentrate on a special place. How do we get people who do not trust us and are trying to overcome and control us to focus on a spot they may not want to return to ?"

Daria smiled at his question. "I knew that would come up sooner or later. Without trying to sound too superior we have overcome that method although it still works. We have developed a technique that bypasses the efforts of the mind. The beauty of this technique is that the individual is not aware of it taking place."

At this point Dan was also smiling. "I was wondering why you didn't appear to be very upset." he remarked.

"Getting them there is not the problem. Keeping them there is going to be a bit tricky. That is why I must return alone to my world." Daria added.

"As I mentioned earlier I will do my best to keep Ian engaged to give you the time you need." Dan said.

"It sounds like a workable plan." smiled Eleanor. "But!."

At the sound of this word both Dan and Daria took on serious expressions.

"It still remains a problem to figure a way to get every one to one place."

Dan remained silent for a few seconds then finally managed; "I got so carried away thinking how well we were doing I forgot about that.

"I think we have all done enough mental strain for one day." remarked Eleanor. "Why not we just relax for the evening, or what's left of it. We have a busy day tomorrow. I will work on getting all concerned together tomorrow. In the meantime you may pour us all another glass of wine."

~ ~ ~ ~ ~ ~

Dan was up and out by nine AM knowing that Daria was transferring to her own world shortly after. He really didn't have a set plan for how to keep Ian occupied but was sure he could play it by ear.

"I guess more inquiries about how the FBI is doing with their study, Ha-Ha." he thought. *"He really is being a sly fox by playing me against Eleanor and Daria and in turn playing them against me. I wonder how long they have been playing this take over game and for what purpose ?"*

Dan arrived at Ian's "FBI" office just before ten. He went through the usual check in procedure and was escorted to Ian's office. He did notice however, that he caught a few people by surprise who suddenly set about as if they were really busy.

Ian jumped up extending his hand along with his put on phony smile.

"I didn't think you would make it."

Dan took his hand with a little extra pressure. "I didn't know if I would myself until this morning. I did a lot of soul searching last night and decided you were probably right. I'm still just a little confused as to why another people would want to take over another planet ?"

"That my friend is the big question, which is why our agency is doing everything possible to discover their intent."

"Well along those lines have you made any decent progress ? Since it's my world naturally I am concerned."

"I'm glad you feel that way and I'm pleased you are on our side. We need more good citizens like you who don't panic easily."

"So far so good." Dan told himself. *"He appears to be buying my made up bull. All I have to do now is kill more time to allow Daria her thing."* Dan was now trying to think of more inquiries to keep Ian occupied. Just then the phone rang. Ian answered sounding like a professional. He gave a quick gaze at Dan and half turned away saying. "Oh yes, that information I have in another office, hold on one moment." Looking again at Dan he quickly mouthed "Excuse me." and walked out of the office. Dan smiled to himself knowing the call was from Eleanor. He could see nothing obvious relating to either the FBI or his planned take over. Dan relaxed and patiently waited.

Ian returned all smiles and appeared more relaxed himself.

"What ever Eleanor fed him apparently satisfied him." Dan reflected.

"Next question." Dan continued. "When you do discover what you think to be useful information, What then ? And how can I be useful ?"

Ian seemed even more pleased with Dan's renewed interest and fudged some answers he thought appropriate. Dan continued his pretend interest in order to kill time. At one PM he made it a point to look at his watch stating,

"Oh wow, I didn't realize it was that late. I should grab a bite of lunch and get to the studio. I still have a business to look after."

Ian smiled at his remark knowing that was where Eleanor said he was going. Dan quickly said his goodbyes and said he would return in two days. He really did have some photo projects to continue. He was glad to be back on the street. He was running out of things to discuss. As he walked to his studio he stopped for a chile dog from one of his favorite street vendors at the same time checking to see if he was being followed. He would have been disappointed if he wasn't. Sure enough he recognized one of the men from the phony office. He smiled to himself as he neared the building that housed his studio. As he entered the lobby he observed his shadow turn around obviously to report back to Ian that Dan was being a good boy.

~ ~ ~ ~

Not to let his business go completely to hell Dan did make some contact with potential clients. He even called Mark Watson, his deadline nemesis, whom he did not particularly care for, but he was always good for some out of the ordinary projects. Killing an appropriate amount of time he closed the studio and headed for home and the two women. He checked twice to make sure he was not being followed and to his comfort all was clear.

He entered his apartment to a very warm loving embrace from Eleanor. He avoided kissing her not to embarrass Daria whom he hoped had returned. Daria exited the bedroom sporting a full face smile. She appeared relaxed and content.

"I gather from the look on your face everything went well today ?"

"It certainly did." she smiled in answer, "I'll fill you in on the details later but right now I would like to celebrate with some of your fantastic wine."

"I'll join you in that." offered Eleanor.

Obviously outnumbered Dan had no objections as he walked to his wine rack choosing a particularly soft red mix. The girls couldn't wait to toast a happy future.

"I appreciate your enthusiasm but it's not over yet." Dan said trying not to be a total downer. Turning to Eleanor and smiling he furthered with, "Your telephone call this morning was perfect timing. Whatever you said to Ian was welcomed news. He did not suspect me in any way other than having my doubts. I'm letting him believe he is slowly winning me over. Now Daria, from the look on your face I take it you had a successful day also."

Beaming like she never had before, Daria excitedly started telling of her day. First and foremost, which was the main cause of her excitement, she had received news that her family were no longer hostages. She had not seen them yet but it was confirmed they were free and clear of any threats of danger. It seems a stranger to them and others overpowered their keeper. "Our tech people were then able to transport the guard back to his own planet with no possibility of return, ever again." She emphasized, her smile widening.

"That's great news Daria." said Eleanor moving to give her a big hug.

Dan had no reservations about opening the wine now. All three happily toasted one another.

"Who was this night in shining armor." asked Eleanor.

"No one knows. Someone suggested he was also being held against his will."

Both Eleanor and Dan sounded the name "JOSH" at the same time. "We can only hope." Eleanor added.

"And to answer your next question we worked it out that no one can return to our planet without us except..."

At this Dan turned instantly serious.

Grinning now Daria went on "Except for whatever we have planned for the group."

Dan and Eleanor now joined her smile.

"It was suggested by one of our tech. group, pending your approval of course, that if you could get them all to transport back to our little settlement which has since been made escape proof, then we could guarantee their transfer to their own home planet without the possibility of reversal."

Eleanor and Dan looked at each other then back to Daria.

"Is this really possible ?" asked Eleanor.

"There's still some fine tuning to be done but we are waiting Dan's approval."

"My approval, why my approval ? You're the one with the advanced knowledge."

"That may be true Dan, but my colleagues back on my world realize you possess certain qualities of knowledge that we seem to have lost over the centuries.

Dan, looking completely lost at her words and feeling a touch chagrined asked the obvious.

"What could I possibly possess that you, in your advanced state, are lacking."

"Eleanor joined in with the answer.

"The spirit to fight, to push back. The spirit to want to maintain your independence even at the expense of your own life. We have not had to do this for many hundreds of years. Living in total peace and harmony has deprived us of that spirit. In this we envy you."

Both women were smiling again but sincere in this thought.

Feeling overwhelmed by these words Dan sat down not knowing what to say. The girls sensing his embarrassment chose to remain silent for a while. They sat opposite him sipping their wine, not looking at him.

Dan was reviewing this whole crazy situation in his mind, finally admitting that in all good conscience he had to see it through now that he has come this far. Feeling this rise of his own confidence again he knew he must accept the challenge and responsibility before him. Looking and speaking softly now Dan addressed his new found companions.

"Forgive me for my selfish misgivings. Of course the answer is yes, you have my approval and my humble thanks for having that much faith in me. I am far from a worker of miracles but I'm sure we can come with a plan to accomplish what we both desire. I will meet with Ian again tomorrow. Daria, you must still remain out of sight. In fact why not transport back to your world and see what you can find out about Josh and see if he was the one who helped. If it is Josh give him my regards and ask him to wait there for us. Give him the full explanation of what we know and have done so far. If he insists on further proof let me know that also and I will transport back there to verify everything. Tell him it is very important and that we need him there if this is to succeed. Eleanor, I think you should make telephone contact with Ian again tomorrow. Arrange to meet him in person if you have to. Convince him that I am buying all his rhetoric. This will help set the stage for us to get him and his cohorts collected in one place. I think I can work out a plan to make this all happen."

Eleanor and Daria appeared to be extremely happy now and even more relaxed than before. Getting their attention once more and with a very serious face Dan asked;

"What's for dinner ?"

$\mathbf{D}$an was answered once again with Eleanor's talent of making something wonderful out of nothing. Thoughts began going through his mind. *"Besides being a good cook, she is intelligent and a very loving person. Something I've been looking for a long time."* Breaking his own mood of fantasy he scolded himself. *"Whoa, back away boy. It won't be long before you're alone again. Just enjoy her company and forget the rest."*

After dinner they all retired to the living room for a relaxing second glass of wine. Dan outlined some thoughts on getting all the "Bad Guys" back to Daria's world at the pre-chosen location.

"In fact I think this idea fits in even better with having Josh there." he said.

"If it even is Josh." cautioned Eleanor.

"You're right, but I'm keeping my fingers crossed." Dan hesitated for a moment thinking then suddenly said. "Try this for size, both of you go back tomorrow."

"Why both ?" asked Eleanor.

"Because you said you already worked with him on the escape plan. He obviously has some trust in you. We're not sure about Daria. Do what is necessary to make contact with him. When you do, fill him in on everything up to date. Emphasize my part in this. I'm sure he will go along with it then. For the short time we had contact I could feel a trust was developed between us."

Eleanor smiled softly, her face lightly flushed showing that ever present admiration for Dan. He was conscious of this but chose to ignor it for now. Other matters had priority.

"Listen carefully, both of you. Here's what I propose. Once contact is made with Josh and he is aware of his part in this I'm sure he will go along with it. When Daria has accomplished all the preparations she spoke of, you, Eleanor, will report to Ian about Josh's escape and the fact that he is starting to incite trouble with the peace loving people. Tell him Daria gave you this information. That he is convincing them to go against Ian's rules. He has already recruited a few who are actually willing to fight physically against Ian and his crew. Convince Ian that he must go back to your world to quell this uprising and that it will take all his people that are presently here. I will try to work my way further into his confidence and persuade him to take me along on this stop the rebellion mission. Once there he can encircle Josh and the rebels and then Daria and her tech people can do their thing."

"And if it doesn't work ?" questioned Daria.

"Then we'll go to plan "B".

"And what is plan "B" ?" Eleanor inquired.

Looking at both women Dan calmly stated;

"I have no idea, so I guess it will just have to work."

They smiled cautiously at his answer.

"Oh yeah, one more thing. When you do see Josh, if it is Josh, tell him not to have too many others with him. Just a few perhaps to make it look real. I will definitely be there and if it does get physical, which I doubt, Josh and I will take care of that part. And if it not Josh, try to ascertain who and from where. If he is from my world outline the same plan for him. For identification I will be wearing an American flag lapel pin on a dark jacket over a light blue shirt and no tie."

"You really are covering all contingencies." remarked Eleanor.

"That's why you're the right one to help our people." added Daria.

"And we won't forget you for this." was said warmly by Eleanor.

Holding eye contact with her for a few seconds Dan then turned away.

"Now for the hard part, can you do this in two days or less.

The gals looked at each other then to Dan.

"Your wish is our command, "O Exalted One" replied a half laughing Eleanor as she bowed from the waist.

"Okay, enough of being serious." Dan commented. "Let's just relax for the rest of the evening. We can go over the fine details tomorrow when we are all more rested. More wine ladies?"

"Are you trying to get us drunk and have your way with us ?" inquired Daria with a grin.

"By no means fair maiden, I just wanted us to relax for a while."

"Too bad." mumbled Eleanor holding her glass out.

The evening was restful and all three turned in early. Dan was particularly tired and started to fall asleep in his chair. The girls took the hint and took their leave.

~ ~ ~ ~ ~ ~

It was after eight when Dan arose to the smell of bacon frying. Eleanor had been especially quiet so as not to disturb Dan's well needed sleep. She kissed him lightly on the cheek as he entered the kitchen. He stopped her as she turned away and kissed her gently on the lips. She smiled and blushed as her eyes met his.

"Good morning." Dan said softly.

Still flushed with emotion. she quietly returned his greeting as they heard Daria approaching. While they ate breakfast Dan quickly reviewed their plans for the day, each having a specific task. After the simple but pleasant meal Dan watched Daria transfer herself to the other world. He himself was going to visit Ian again to get whatever information he could that may help him finalize his plans. Eleanor would call Ian again to report in on Dan's behavior. With a quick hug Eleanor said good bye to Dan as he left the apartment. She was trying very hard not to be too emotional

Dan really did not want to see Ian again yet he knew he must keep up the charade if nothing else. When he arrived at the "FBI" office he was not subjected to the usual check in procedure. He was directed right to Ian's office. The supervisor was also there. Dan had not seen him since the very first meeting. The high fallutin boss act had been done away with and Gary Curtis was actually friendly. Thinking to himself, Dan was pleased his act must have been somewhat believable. There was obviously more acceptance of him. Dan started with his made up lies again hoping to learn more.

"You know Ian, I was thinking on the way here and came up with a scenario that sort of puzzled me and I must admit frightened me a little."

"Oh !" answered Ian.

Dan knew he caught the interest of both Gary and Ian.

"And what would that be ?" continued Ian.

"Well I was wondering are you prepared for any aggressive behavior from these so called peaceful people.

Gary and Ian smiled looking at each other. Gary spoke first.

"I think you need not worry about such things. We have done many studies of these people. They hardly know what the word weapon even means." "Then how do they control others ?" asked Dan.

"Simple fear and intimidation." Ian took over. "These two things have been quite successful in their handling of others."

Dan could easily tell he was referring to their own take over procedures. He also thought to himself, while laughing internally, *"it has worked up until now."*

"That's good to know." Dan replied excitedly. "Obviously you people always have your weapons with you."

Dan detected a slight change in both faces. He took this to mean just what he figured. They did not possess weapons. At least that's the chance he was going to take until he learned otherwise.

"When do we move in on the group that is already here ?" Remember this is my world and I want to keep it free."

His enthusiasm saying these words was casting it's spell on both "FBI" men. Dan no sooner gazed at the wall clock reading ten thirty when Ian's phone rang. He knew it was Eleanor when Gary urged him out of the room on the pretense of showing him something. It wasn't long when Ian joined them at the map table all smiles. Either Eleanor did a great job of fooling Ian or he was just sold down the river. He chose not to believe the latter. Satisfied that he was well accepted he made excuses about going to the studio to catch up on some work. As he was leaving he thought he recognized Daria in the far corner of the large room. Dan pretended not to see and acted normal as he left. He hoped she maintained the fortitude to successfully go through with her part. He would find out tonight. He left for the studio and was not followed.

~ ~ ~ ~

Safely tucked away in his studio Dan was still haunted by the sight of Daria in Ian's complex. He knew he would have to wait until tonight to get the full story.

Dan had a few walk in inquiries and was glad for the distraction. A call from his sister regarding watching Billy for a few days added to his mind's confusion. He politely begged off using work commitments as an excuse. Perhaps in a couple of weeks they could get together. He was not comfortable deceiving his sister but she would not understand his situation at all. She already thinks he's a bit odd. No matter, he knew he would make it up to young Billy.

Just after five he locked the door and walked home stopping for some wine.

As he entered his apartment Eleanor ran to him enfolding him in her arms along with a passionate kiss.

"I guess Daria's not back yet ?" Dan inquired.

"You really know how to spoil a girls mood." Eleanor pouted and the added, "She should be here soon. More wine I see, are you sure you're not trying to corrupt us with your evil ways ?" She was grinning the whole time she said this.

"That would not be proper for a gentleman to do." replied Dan trying to sound serious.

"That's too bad." Eleanor mumbled.

"Did you say something ?"

Looking up at him she answered softly, "No, not really."

"Oh." Dan said as he went to put the wine on the table.

Minutes later Daria appeared on the sofa grinning from ear to ear.

"What's got you so happy ?" inquired Eleanor also smiling.

"Nothing special." replied Daria. "Nothing except that every detail of Dan's plan seem to be falling in place."

Dan and Eleanor turned to each other looking pleased and excited. Daria went on almost ignoring them both.

"First and very important is the fact that the transport technicians have improved our transport system which they now promise me is foolproof. Secondly they have the perfect spot for Ian's group to transport to which is fully secured. There will be no escape from it. Even with some of us present only those specific people of Ian's group will be transported with a guarantee of no return. It will be our job now to get those chosen, together in one place and let Ian think he is controlling the transference."

Daria's excitement increased with her persistent talking.

"I made contact with my family and everyone is fine. And some of the best news of all is the knight in shining armor was Josh."

By now Daria was talking so fast Eleanor had to make her pause and take a deep breath.. Daria laughingly apologized but resumed talking again.

"I spoke with Josh at length and he believed all I told him. Particularly about you. He was pleased you took up where he left off, not by his own choosing, and yes, he will stay on my world as you requested and meet you as you planned. He thought your rebellion idea was great. He will be all set when ever you are."

By now all three were beaming with joyful satisfaction.

"I'm glad I purchased more wine, we can all celebrate tonight."

Eleanor's smile grew even broader upon hearing this.

"Wait, I'm not finished yet. Josh told me something that really set me back. It was something I had been longing for but wasn't aware it existed."

Dan and Eleanor stared back at Daria with questioning eyes.

"Now that things are looking to improve for us, Josh admitted to wanting to know me better. So much so that he may chose to stay with us when this whole nightmare is finally ended. I can't tell you how happy that made me. I tried to be friendly with him which was very difficult given the circumstances of my family and all."

Hearing this, Eleanor moved closer to Dan hooking her arm in his. Daria noticed Eleanor's move saying with a hugh grin;

"Now you two don't have to be so secretive because of me."

Dan blushed slightly while Eleanor smiled even more. Daria finally ended with, Yes, I would love a glass of wine."

Dan took the hint and proceeded to un cork the wine while Eleanor retrieved the glasses. Once the wine had been poured Dan gave Daria a warm hug.

"I'm so happy for you and I will make sure the rest of our plan works."

Daria smiled with tears in her eyes. Eleanor followed suit then the three toasted to success.

Dan was a bit disturbed that she had not mentioned meeting with Ian today. Was this all an act and should he be cautious about what he says from here on out ? Dan no sooner finished this thought when Daria set her glass down.

"I'm glad you did not react today when you saw me at Ian's work place. Ian still believes I'm back at my world and had been trying to get in touch with me.."

Dan felt a sudden relief come over him.

"I went there to give him the first warning of the stirring of discontent. He did seem concerned. We will have to keep a close eye on him."

"Good." Dan replied. "That fits in well with my discussion today with him. Okay let's set the big move for day after tomorrow. That will give us and him time to gather all his agents who are on this world. Unfortunately that will have to include you, Eleanor."

"I'm aware of that and I am prepared. Between Daria and I, I believe we can convince him of the danger of a rebellion and that we must be there to squash it. Especially with Josh sort of being a leader. Because Josh comes from your world I'm sure even Ian could appreciate his inherent danger to his take over mission."

Dan felt a sense of pride in Eleanor, actually in both women, who were not in the habit of fighting for their freedom. He was now truly confident this would work.

Okay tomorrow, let's plan on getting another warning or two to Ian. I will also meet with him again and work on getting all the people gathered. I hope to convince him to let me go along also."

"If not." said Daria, "You can transport by yourself. I will arrange that as soon as I get there tomorrow."

"That's a great idea, that would really be a big help. That way I don't have to worry about any sudden repercussions from Ian if he suddenly realizes I'm not on his side."

"Just be careful." cautioned Daria. "Ian does possess abilities above and beyond the normal person. Which is why, I guess, he is one of the leaders."

"If they don't let me go along with them, is it possible to transport me so that I'm there as they get there."

"That is no problem. I will have your signal pre programmed to do just that. "I can't wait for this to be over so I can go home where I belong. No offense, Dan, but this is not my home and family."

"None taken Daria. Trust me this is going to work."

Eleanor moved closer and gave Daria a quick squeeze.

Okay ladies, a little wine and then dinner. It will be a busy and tedious day tomorrow and we must keep clear heads."

"Didn't I tell you Daria, he's nothing but a party pooper." said Eleanor, of course with a big smile.

Both girls laughed. Dan faked being insulted and stomped off to the kitchen. The girls laughed even harder. He did not return right away, so Eleanor went to see if he really was angry. She found him busy preparing dinner.

"You're such a joy." She said as she hugged him from behind.

"Watch it young lady, things like that could lead you into trouble."

"Oh, I hope so." she hugged harder.

Suddenly a voice rang out from the living room.

"Hey you two, it's getting hungry in here."

~ ~ ~

The evening went quickly with all asleep early. Eleanor was up before the others fixing breakfast for Dan. Daria had already departed for the other world. Dan ate quickly and with a quick kiss left Eleanor pouting.

Dan's first stop was to his studio. He checked his messages and prepared a sign saying **"Temporarily closed due to a family emergency"** He laughed to himself as he tacked it on the door. *"It really is an emergency but in this case the family is the whole planet."*

Once Dan was sure everything was secure, he casually, to kill some time, made his way to the "FBI" office.

Ian appeared to be preoccupied. From the way he was acting Dan assumed Eleanor had already called. That preoccupied look was actually worry he figured. Good, so far things were falling into place. Ian with a half smile asked Dan to wait in his office.

"I need to talk with Gary, something just came up."

Dan waited close to ten minutes when Ian returned appearing to be less uptight.

"Ah Dan, glad you're still here. There has been much discussion since you left yesterday. We are going to act on your suggestion and start a round up of these other world agents. Just for questioning of course. We will offer the proverbial olive branch and try to ascertain the purpose of their mission. I might even arrange to have them transported back to their world."

"Can you do that." asked Dan with an air of excitement and curiosity while acting like a school boy.

"I'm sure I can arrange something. I managed to build up some faithful contacts on the other world. I believe I can still count on their cooperation." Ian answered smugly.

"I wouldn't count on that." Dan's thoughts ran threw his mind.

"That would be great for us, perhaps you can arrange for them to stay there." Dan continued with fake enthusiasm. "Could I go along with you, I sure would like to be in on the end of this takeover to know that my planet would now be safe again."

"Gary and I did discuss that very idea but decided against such a move. Your patriotism is to be commended but you should leave such dangerous matters up to the professionals."

Dan acted out being disappointed as convincing as possible.

"Well at least could I possibly help with the roundup here. Just to make sure you get every one."

"Even that may be a little too dangerous. Remember we are dealing with an advanced people here. Who knows what they may be capable of. We don't need any innocent people getting hurt."

"I see your point." Dan replied rather sadly. How about Eleanor, I can personally escort her here. I'm sure she won't suspect me. I think she even likes me."

Ian hesitated a moment as if in thought.

"Well, alright, I guess that much would be okay. I know how much you want to help."

"Great, how about I get her here by eight in the morning ?" Dan said, his excitement soaring again.

"I think nine o'clock would be more in order with our plans."

"Nine AM it is. I'm looking forward to this." Dan finalized as he moved for the door. *I'm looking forward to this more than you realize.*"

Ian was all smiles as he watched Dan leave.

Dan did not go directly home. He went across the street to watch from a second floor window. He could sit and watch the comings and goings of the "FBI". He didn't have to wait to long. As he thought, three of Ian's workers left the building heading in different directions. Dan thumbed through some magazines killing time. After an hour and a half, sure that there was no other major actions across the street, he casually left the book store winding his way to his apartment.

He stopped at a flower vendor on the street and bought one red rose. He started to walk away but changed his mind and purchased another. After all he was still dealing with two women. It was early afternoon when he entered his apartment. Both women were there.

Eleanor gave her usual loving hug while Daria was all smiles. As if on Que all three began speaking at once. Dan threw up both his hands laughing.

"Okay, I know when I'm outnumbered. You first Daria."

Without hesitation she started.

"I believe we have everything set. Your personal signal has been established and we can transport you on your signal."

"Will that be the site of the gathering ?" Dan inquired.

"Absolutely, and Josh and two others will be waiting there. And to anticipate your next question, He mentioned that he is also ready for any signs of physical resistance. He said he is almost looking forward to it. He indicated that you would understand."

"Indeed I do."smiled Dan."What about the two volunteers ?"

"They have been instructed to stand clear if anything does happen. Our transport system is fully prepared for action once we are positive all are present. You will also be transported seconds before the group."

"That sounds great. I can't wait to see the expression on Ian's face when I greet him."

Daria then turned serious.

"Do you think there will be anything physical ?" She asked with a worried expression.

"No, I really don't think they are prepared for any good old fashioned American physical resistance. If it does happen I promise you I will look after Josh."

Hearing Dan's answer she took on a full blush.

"Does it show that much."

Dan smiled as Eleanor hugged her warmly. Gazing up at Dan, her eyes told him what was in her heart.

Getting back on track Dan, in a firm voice said;

"Okay, Eleanor you're next."

Smiling she said; "I made two phone calls to Ian, with warnings of a resistance group growing. He appeared to be quite concerned and is definitely leaning to go there with a group to quell the disturbance. Then I reported that you were being a good boy. He told me to keep pace with every move you make."

She finished with her usual smile.

"Now me." Dan stated. "I believe he absolutely is convinced of my sincerity, and how anxious I want to be part of his group. However, He will not let me go along with him. It would bee too dangerous for me."

The women gave a half laugh at this.

"Now the difficult part. I promised Ian I would personally hand deliver you to him at nine o"clock tomorrow morning."

"Oh, you mean I get to go out with you in public. Oh goody." She smiled.

Dan half smiled at her reaction. "I'm trying to be serious here."

"I know you are." she answered. "I'm sorry." still smiling.

"I hope you're acting is up to par. You have to be convincing that you were just betrayed."

Eleanor stood and in a raised voice, started; "Why you no good rat, how could you. I thought I meant something to you. All this time you were deceiving me."

Now Daria had a serious look of shock. She immediately became frightened. There was even a hint of a tear in the corner of her eye.

Eleanor noticed this and instantly went to her side showing a big smile.

"I guess I am convincing." she said gazing at Dan.

"You even had me frightened." he laughed.

"Will I do." Eleanor calmly inquired.

"I think you passed the test. Now, how about something to eat, I'm starved."

"I'm sure we can find some rotten cheese for the big rat." she replied getting up and pulling Daria with her.

~ ~ ~ ~

Dinner was both happy and quiet. Personal thoughts of the next day occupied every ones mind. Daria appeared to be particularly preoccupied. Dan picked up on this and quietly suggested she transport back to her world and spend some time with her family and Josh.

"Do you really think I should ? Could I ?"

"You have done more than your part in this little scheme. You already know what has to be done tomorrow. We'll both see you in the morning."

"Thank you." she whispered through tears.

Dan held Eleanor's hand as they watched her fade away. Eleanor immediately swung around putting her arms around Dan followed with a kiss.

"You're so nice." she whispered. "And yes I will be good tonight. I know we have a full day tomorrow but you better watch out when this is all over."

"Is that a threat young lady ?"

"You bet it is." Eleanor answered.

Thoughts of losing her tomorrow crept into the dark recesses of Dan's subconscious. Bringing himself back to reality he broke the embrace.

"Let me help you clean up then we can relax for the evening."

"Do they make all men like you or are you just special." she whispered.

Dan ignored her words starting to clear the table. Deep inside he knew he was falling in love with her and knew it was a mutual thing but he was heeding his own council to stay at arms length. After tomorrow she would be gone. He tried ignoring his feelings to make tomorrow less painful. Eleanor sensed a change in his demeanor but decided to leave him alone for now.

Chapter 18

Dan and Eleanor were both up early with Dan still acting on the cool side. Eleanor chose not to push the issue, at least not now. It was the wrong timing. At eight thirty they made ready for the trip to the "FBI" office.

"Just in case we are being watched act friendly on the way, but not overly friendly. When we get to Ian's place of dirty business you can go into your act when you think the time is appropriate.

The pair left the apartment setting their course for Ian's office.

"Are you up to this ?" Dan asked.

"You bet I am, especially knowing that you are on our side." Eleanor answered with her usual smile.

Dan reenforced his promise.

"I will not let anything happen to you."

They arrived at eight fifty six at the "FBI" office.

"What are we doing here ?" Eleanor said loud and clear as they entered. Ian was there, all smiles.

"I'm delivering the package as promised." Dan spoke as he urged Eleanor closer with a gentle push on her back.

"Hello Eleanor, good to see you again." Ian said through a beaming smile.

Eleanor slowly shifted into her academy award act. She looked at Dan confused. She whipped her head to Ian again then back to Dan.

"Hey, what's going on. I thought we had a thing going ?"

"Perhaps you did, but Ian seems to indicate that you are not the person I first thought you were."

Again she looked at Ian with hate in her eyes.

"So you have been lying to me all along. You told me you needed my help to win over this jerk and now you double cross me. I'm out of here."

She tried moving towards the door but two of Ian's henchmen blocked her.

Ian extending his hand stated;

"Well, you kept your part of the bargain so I guess that will be all for now."

Dan took the offered hand politely.

"Good luck with your roundup."

"What round up." yelled Eleanor

Dan exited, concerned, of course, yet also felt that Eleanor could handle the uncomfortable situation.

As soon as Dan closed the door Ian addressed Eleanor.

"Nice act you put up, you almost made me feel like the bad guy, but I'm glad you're here. We will need all the help we can get to counter this so called rebellion."

"How many were you able to get hold of ?" asked Eleanor.

"I believe we have everyone. You were the last.'

"Good, and I believe Daria is expecting us."

"That's correct, I spoke to her earlier and she has managed to get these so called rebels gathered in one place. Our transport time is set for nine thirty so lets get to the big room where the others are waiting."

Eleanor followed Ian down the hall to the so called Map room

True enough there were many there. Without making it too obvious she made a quick count.

"Looks good." she told herself. *"I don't believe anyone is missing."*.

A minute or so later Ian spoke out.

"Okay folks, this is it. Prepare yourselves. I don't expect trouble but you never know. Gather closer."

At exactly nine thirty the transfer took place.

~ ~ ~

At nine twenty seven Dan thought of transporting, then the next thing he knew he was staring at Josh and his extended hand. They shook hands warmly.

"I knew you would finish what I started."

Dan doubled his smile when he saw Daria walking towards them.

"Thank you," he offered as Josh pulled him back to the fringes of the welcoming sight.

On time twenty warm bodies appeared not knowing what to expect. Ian's face was priceless as he observed both Josh and Dan smiling. One of the "FBI" men made a move towards Dan who almost automatically put forth a left jab squarely to the jaw of his attacker. Almost down a few of the others caught him before he hit the ground. By now Josh had stepped forward ready for action. This however did not occur.

"Try your influence on someone else." Dan said as he nodded to Daria who in turn spoke into a small silver box. Like magic the whole gang disappeared. Daria spoke again into her magic silver box. Within seconds she received a reply. Turning to the remaining people with an ear to ear smile.

"That's it folks, the nightmare is over. We will never see them again, at least not for a few hundred years."

Eleanor rushed to Dan throwing her arms around him.

"Thank you my darling, this was a wonderful thing you did."

Dan felt as she did but was a bit bashful of a public exhibition.

Sensing his embarrassment Eleanor withdrew from the hug but stayed with her arm hooked in his. Looking to Daria, Dan asked,

"What's now involved with getting Josh and I back home and you can be on your way with no further worries."

"What's your hurry pal ? Relax and let's enjoy a few days of peace before we get serious again."

Eleanor and Daria agreed with Josh whole heartily.

"Once again I can see when I'm outnumbered. I guess a few more days would be okay, but I do have a business to tend to."

Eleanor gave a extra warm squeeze to Dan's arm.

Chapter 19

The quant country setting was the same except the café' was closed. The woman who ran the Café' was now walking slowly, hand in hand with Dan heading for the Worry Free Inn. No one was around to see Dan and Eleanor enter the last cabin Dan had occupied for the last few months. Dan was a little shy with Eleanor's instant advances. Not that he didn't have the same feelings, he just felt that things would move a little more slowly. Swept away with the emotions of desire he met her advances with equal enthusiasm..

They slept comfortably in each others arms until the birds, up with the sun, welcomed another day. Come on sleepy head we're supposed to meet Daria and Josh by the village green. A quick cup of coffee interrupted by a few loving hugs from Eleanor and the pair were soon on their way to town.

As they approached the green Dan could see the park was already buzzing with activity. The closer they were, the more warning bells went off in Dan's head. He thought he recognized a few of the people. He could feel himself beginning to tense up and as he did he could feel Eleanor's hand tighten on his. Within twenty feet of the circular bandstand it happened. Dan spotted Ian and a few others from the "FBI" office. He quickly pulled his hand away from Eleanor only to find her grabbing his arm with both hands. It was not only Ian he recognized but every one else that had been part of the transfer scheme.

"Hey, what's is this ?" he said rather loudly.

"Calm down." Eleanor answered sweetly, "everything will be okay."

As Dan looked around he could feel a strange sensation come over him at the same time he noticed a faint shimmer of light surround him. Eleanor had now let go of his arm. He was free to move. He soon found out that movement was limited. He seemed to be encased in a diameter of approximately a six foot circle of nothing that he could visually detect, yet his moves were restricted to the circle. Reaching out trying to feel his restraining wall his arms reached only so far before resistance was felt.

Dan turned to Eleanor, a look of betrayal covering his face, his eyes filled with questions.

Daria stepped forward. "Obviously you want some sort of explanation."

"I most certainly do." Dan said forcefully.

"You have been a case study test for us. I must admit we are very pleased with the results you have showed us. We did not expect a civilization as primitive as yours to possess such strong survival instincts as a people."

Now Dan was becoming confused.

"Primitive ? Us primitive ? he thought.

"Yes" Daria answered his thoughts. "We have been studying your planet for some time now, but your intellectual growth has been extremely slow. We feel, perhaps, it is because the inhabitants of your world are always preoccupied with dominating each other. There appears not to be an effort for peaceful coexistence."

Trying to maintain some poise Dan spoke up.

"That's all well and good to have your own opinions, but what has that got to do with me ? Why am I being confined ?"

"That's for your own safety." smiled Eleanor. "Your independence and willingness to fight to keep that freedom we felt could put your safety in jeopardy. It's okay my love we will keep you safe."

"What am I now a prisoner on this parallel world of yours."

"That's an inappropriate word to use. We prefer to say a subject of study."

"A rose by any other name." Dan mumbled.

"Did you say something." Eleanor asked.

"Not really, you wouldn't understand."

Dan resigned himself to his confinement, at least at the moment.

Ian walked by; "Good to see you again. Glad to have you with us. You have been a most interesting study so far."

Dan just glared at him.

"Okay Dan, just calm down and collect your thoughts. I'm sure you can come up with some sort of a way out of this." He ran these thoughts through his mind quickly, hoping no one was tuned into him.

One by one people moved away leaving only Josh, Daria and

Eleanor. Dan remained silent, looking and thinking. The remaining trio moved closer. Daria, who appeared to be a leader spoke pleasantly.

"It has been decided to move you to more permanent housing. You will be given all the comforts that you are accustomed to. You will soon be able to relax more. Have patience with us. No harm will come to you."

Dan turned to Eleanor, eyes pleading. She just smiled in answer. Before he realized it he was in front of a small four room cottage surrounded by what he estimated to be a one and a half acre split rail fence.

"This will be your new home. If you need anything additional just ask." Josh stated then turned and walked away.

Daria spoke again and softly; "We will talk later." As she and Eleanor turned and also strolled away.

Naturally the first thing Dan did was to test the perimeter fencing. Like his smaller cage at the bandstand, there was no way to penetrate this invisible wall. He took note of many other small housing units. Some with what appeared to be slightly different themes of background. His brain working overtime he made the assumption that they also housed specimens most likely from other planets. Accepting this limitation, at least for the moment, Dan turned to and entered the cottage. He was most surprised by what he found. The cottage was furnished and decorated as his own apartment. The kitchen was well supplied with all things he was accustomed to. A stove, microwave, refrigerator and a dishwasher were there for his use. There was a small but well stocked wine rack in the living room. The two remaining rooms were also well appointed. The bedroom and bath were combined. A small library, writing room completed the forth room.

Dan tried to collect his thoughts, then remembered a small veranda outside supplied with a rocking chair. He went outside and deposited himself in the rocker letting go a big sigh.

"Now what ?" he said aloud.

Dan sat comfortably for a while just observing things around him. He noticed movement at a distant cottage. Not really a cottage in a direct sense but a housing complex of sorts. The figure that drew his attention did not exactly look like a human form that he was used to. It appeared smaller in stature and Dan could not quite make out the attire, if that was what it was.

"Another subject of study." he thought, *"from who knows what galaxy."*

Reflecting now on how this whole thing came about, he thought perhaps in the future he should rein in his curiosity. Knowing himself though he knew that would never happen.

The next step, obviously was not his. He would have to wait to see what was in store for him. Suddenly realizing he was hungry Dan walked to the kitchen. He looked in the refrigerator thinking about the food.

Could it contain some kind of drug to control him. Dan closed the fridge and sat at the table thinking.

"Why do I have to have such an overactive imagination. On one hand I have to sustain my body in order to remain clearheaded.. On the other hand, I'm sure they would want to control my independence and aggressiveness."

Dan finally decided on eating to keep up his strength. If they wanted to study him he figured they would want him as normal as possible.

"It may be a rationalization on my part but let's face it, I'm hungry."

Back to the fridge again he chose bacon and eggs for himself.

He knew it was close to his normal supper time but right now bacon and eggs seemed to foot the bill.

He was not bothered the rest of that night. After eating he went outside again and tested the perimeter invisibility. There was no open area. He observed lights slowly coming on in other dwellings. Dan retired for the night. He knew there was nothing he could do that night. The bed was amazingly comfortable and much to his surprise he slept well through the whole night.

After what Dan considered an adequate breakfast he took a second cup of coffee out to the veranda and plopped himself in the rocker to think.

Dan spoke out loud though quietly, baring his thoughts to no one except himself and a few birds.

"Lets review this whole thing from the beginning. I willed myself here to get away from the rat race of the city. I used my mind to get away and found my ideal world. Or did I. Perhaps it wasn't just my mind. Possibly I was just a conduit for their transfer system."

Dan set his coffee cup down, relaxed and thought of home in his park with the pigeons. He pictured himself feeding the nuisance birds.

He enjoyed the scene in his mind but that's all it was. A scene in his mind. Nothing else happened. A transfer did not take place.

He opened his eyes and retrieved his coffee cup.

"I guess that answers my question. The transport had to be all their doing. Either that or it's a grand game of mind control." Dan paused for a moment. "Now you're being silly. I've done enough reading to know it's possible. Perhaps not on the scale I've just gone through, nevertheless the possibility exists. Okay genius, what's the next step ?"

Dan's mind went blank for the moment. Actually more than a moment. More like twenty minutes. He had drifted back to a photo shoot of a few months ago which involved a pretty woman who reminded him of Eleanor. He laughed to himself thinking for the first time in years he felt this attraction to someone and look how it turned out.

As if on Que, Dan looked up only to see Eleanor smiling. It took a few seconds to register but Daria was also with her. Dan's gaze upon Eleanor was not exactly one of fondness.

"How was your sleep period?" inquired Daria.

"Under the circumstances I managed to do well and to now ask the obvious, When do I leave here ?"

Daria smiled politely but coldly answered;

"We have not yet finished our study."

Dan threw back just as coldly.

"I guess you didn't learn anything in the last couple of months."

His answer triggered a smile in Eleanor.

"I wouldn't exactly say that."

Dan turned to Eleanor surprised by her comment.

"You mean that was more than a case study." he asked sarcastically

Replying matter- of -factly, Eleanor said.

"Oh, it was a study of the reproductive habits of your species but I must admit there were some pleasurable side effects." She smiled after saying this. Daria joined in her smile.

"Glad to have helped in your study." Dan replied coldly. I feel like such a fool to have fallen for all your lies. I must admit though both of your performances, in fact everyone's play acting was phenomenal. I really am the fool for being taken in so completely. That's what I get for trusting people I don't know. I feel so betrayed." Looking directly to Eleanor he added, "And to think I actually started to fall for you. Why couldn't you have just asked your questions openly."

Daria chose to answer.

"We have tried that in the past but the results were not accurate enough. Once beings know that we are a more advanced species their behavior is no longer unrehearsed. Therefore the information we are gathering does not answer our questions well enough for us to gauge whether we can assist in your growth or not."

"That almost makes sense." he thought to himself. Dan speaking directly now,

"Why did you feel it necessary to put me through what you just did ?"

"We found your spirit of independence rather interesting." Eleanor answered. "We ourselves may have had that ions ago but we have no recollection of that. We found it truly unique and wanted to see it in action."

"And did I pass your test ?" Dan asked sarcastically again.

Eleanor, staying calm answered,

"You were a most interesting study. Your independence streak is very strong. Stronger than we anticipated, which is why our study was extended beyond normal. We even sense that now you still reside in a rebellious state."

"That's an understatement if I ever heard one." Dan spat back.

"That's what makes you such an ideal study." joined Daria. "We would like to know what drives this necessity for such behavior."

"I feel sorry for you then." Dan answered in a genuine tone. "For as advanced as you claim to be you appear to have missed the boat."

Daria and Eleanor were now looking confused.

"Freedom." Dan said emphatically. "Freedom to think as you please. Freedom to do what you chose as long as it does not affect others in a harmful way. Freedom without restrictions of any kind. Freedom to just be me." Looking directly at the two women, "Can you even fathom that sort of idea ? Have you lost that much of yourselves in your advanced state of intelligence ? Think about yourselves, then think of me."

Dan turned and walked back into the house calling over his shoulder, "Have a better day ladies. Let me know when I can go home ?"

He entered the house smiling to himself, leaving both women with questioning expressions.

All I can do is hope now. Hope that they will understand and heed what I said and release me to my world and they can depart with their world thinking about what they are missing in life. Talk about the grass always being greener. My grass is more than adequate now that I've seen the other not mush greener grass.

Dan quietly rested with a cup of coffee letting the two women have their time to reflect on what he said. A half hour passed and he peeked out the window. The girls were no where to be seen. Softly laughing to himself Dan grabbed a book and went out to the small porch. Putting his feet up he relaxed with the adventures of Huckleberry Finn. In between reading and dozing he was suddenly aware that he had company. What was now his four not so favorite people. Looking up Dan asked softly but sarcastically;

"And to what do I owe the honor of this visit by the four horseman." His reference, of course was over their heads.

Daria again in the part of spokesperson took the lead.

"We have an offer to make to you and please hear us out completely before you answer."

Dan looked intently at all four faces and spoke softly.

"I'm listening."

Daria began their presentation but his eyes were only on Eleanor who was staring back with a loving smile.

"I wish it could have been." he thought.

"We are proposing two choices. First, and this is the one we hope you choose, is that we will arrange for you to move freely about and interact with us in any way you wish. Of course during this time we will continue our study observations. This would last as long as necessary for us to learn what motivates this freedom you so dearly cherish, at which time you will be transported to where ever you wish, or if you choose, you can stay on our world."

"And choice number two ?" Dan inquired without hesitation.

Daria looked to the other three who all nodded in the affirmative to proceed.

"You may choose to go back to your world now. We will return you to your park bench and pigeons."

She smiled at her own remarks.

After only a slight pause Eleanor spoke.

"Of course if you choose our first option you could also further study us, up close and personal."

She emphasized these last words in a very soft, almost intimate voice. Her offer was obvious to Dan.

"That is a tempting offer, to learn more of these people." he told himself. *"But then again what do I do with the knowledge I gain. I'm a nobody and because of that no one in the Government would believe me. I would most likely be branded a nut job and be put away. Who would blame them. The parallel world theory is just that. A theory known only to a handful of quantum theorists. Most of whom would also brand me as a nut job."*

"Your offer is extremely tempting."

Hearing this Eleanor sported a loving smile which soon disappeared.

"But I have nothing to gain from such a study. If you are going to be true to your word I chose option number two.

Even Ian and Josh appeared disappointed with his answer. Dan turned to Eleanor, tears in her eyes.

"I'm sorry but it just wouldn't work. I don't fit in here."

Daria disappointed accepted his words and calmly mouthed the words, "So be it".

She spoke into her small communicator. The next thing Dan saw was his favorite pigeons vying for position at his feet. He looked around both happy and sad. He was home. He was back in the big, crowded city.

"The rat race would still be the same." he thought. *"But that part I can change. At least I learned that much from this adventure."* He laughed at his own thoughts. *"If I had thought about this logically before hand I would already be set up happily in some small town. Oh well, it's never too late."*

He left his favorite bench heading home to his apartment, first stopping at a street vendor for a chile dog.

~ ~ ~ ~ ~ ~

"It is good to be home. My own home." thought Dan. He unlocked and pushed the door open only to notice the lights on in the kitchen, his nose detecting something very good cooking. Dan froze in place eyes scanning the room. Movement from the kitchen area drew his attention. Eleanor, with an extremely timid expression slowly emerged through the kitchen portal.

"I hope you're not too angry." She said almost in a whisper. Dan stood there in disbelief struggling to find his voice.

"I thought you people said you would leave me alone."

"Yes, that was the promise and they kept their word."

"But what about you ? Don't you keep your promises ?"

Moving a little closer Eleanor continued.

"Oh, but I did."

Confusion showed on Dan's face.

"My world is gone. Cohesion was broken and the planet is continuing its orbit to who knows where."

Dan found himself warming to the idea of Eleanor being in his life. And you ?" he inquired.

"Against the wishes of others I chose to join your world."

She could read the why in his eyes and smiled.

"This may sound strange to you, but I love you. I genuinely love you and want to be with you. I don't care which world It's on."

Dan moved to Eleanor enfolding her in a bear hug. She put her head to his shoulder, tears running down her cheek.

"Can I stay, please." she pleaded.

"Of course you can stay. I don't know how long it would have taken me to adjust to not having you with me. But what were you going to do if I didn't want you ? You gave up your home, you gave up your whole life."

"I knew the risk but to me it was worth trying."

"Will you ever be able to go back to your world ?"

"Not very likely. Our planets won't be this close again for at least two hundred thousand years. I really don't want to wait that long." she joked.

Dan held her away from him slightly so he could look directly into her eyes.

"I'm glad you're here and yes I love you just as much."

Eleanor gave him a lingering kiss then remembered the dinner she was preparing.

"I think I"m burning our dinner."

The End

References

The Fabric of the Cosmos

by Brian Green

Pub; Alfred A. Knopf

Strange Matters

by Tom Siegfried

Pub; Joseph Henry Press

Parallel Worlds

by Michio Kaku

Pub; Doubleday

The Universe Next Door

by Marcus Chown

Pub; Oxford university Press

Also by Author

<u>Simple Short Stories</u>

$\Big($To tingle the Imagination$\Big)$

<u>Simple Short Stories II</u>

$\Big($To further Tingle the Imagination$\Big)$

<u>The Dead Living Mummy</u>

$\Big($An epic Story of a lost

City that ended with a lost mind$\Big)$

<u>The Innocent Murder</u>

$\Big($The Tranquility of an English Manor

upset by a sudden death$\Big)$

<u>The Ancient Ones</u>

$\Big($Another adventure with Eric Dexter$\Big)$

<u>The Librarian Checked Out</u>

$\Big($Murder by the Book?$\Big)$

~ ~ ~ ~

<u>Children's Stories</u>

$\left(\text{A series of eight stories}\right)$

1-The Garden Mystery

2-The Christmas Garland Mystery

3- The New Land

4- New Friends

5- Squiggy and the Bear

6-Squiggy and the Storm

7-The Next Generation

8- Squiggy's Maine Vacation

www.ingramcontent.com/pod-product-compliance
Lightning Source LLC
Chambersburg PA
CBHW031945110726
47902CB00001B/297